Praise for Sarah Salway's *Th...*

"Salway is original, witty, and wise. *The ABCs of Love* defines life, love, and loss with humor and grace."

— CARA LOCKWOOD, author of
I Do (But I Don't)

"Warm and witty, Salway's debut makes learning your ABCs a pleasure."

— LYNN MESSINA, author of
Fashionistas and *Tallulahland*

"More than the sum of its parts—heartbreaking, hilarious, and compulsively readable."

— SARAH MLYNOWSKI, author of
Milkrun, Fishbowl, and *As Seen on TV*

The ABCs
of Love

sarah salway

To my Buddy, Ann!
With love
Sarah x
July 2004

BALLANTINE BOOKS • NEW YORK

The ABCs of Love is a work of fiction. Names, places, and incidents are the products of the author's imagination or are used fictitiously. Any resemblance to actual events, locales, or persons, living or dead, is entirely coincidental.

A Ballantine Book
Published by The Random House Publishing Group

Copyright © 2004 by Sarah Salway

All rights reserved under International and Pan-American Copyright Conventions. Published in the United States by The Random House Publishing Group, a division of Random House, Inc., New York.

Ballantine and colophon are registered trademarks of Random House, Inc.

Originally published in Great Britain by Bloomsbury Publishing Plc in 2004 under the title *Something Beginning With*.

www.ballantinebooks.com

Library of Congress Control Number is available from the publisher upon request.

ISBN 0-345-46703-5

Text design by Cassandra J. Pappas

Manufactured in the United States of America

First Edition: May 2004

10 9 8 7 6 5 4 3 2 1

*For all the generous women I am lucky enough to call my friends,
especially Kay, Annemarie, Debbie, Marnie, Lynne, and Ali.
And for Alice, with respect.*

acknowledgments

Grateful thanks to Anne Hay, Rob Middlehurst, Sheenagh Pugh, Jenny Newman, and James Friel for generously passing on their knowledge and enthusiasm; to Alex Patterson and Esther Dermott for being the hardest act to follow; to Robert Doyle, Mo McAuley, Gaye Jee, Malcolm Lewis, Frank Dullaghan, Victor Tapner, and Shaun Levin for supportive reading; to Allison Dickens for much valued expertise and support; to my agent Rupert Heath, without whom; and of course, to my family, always, for everything.

The alphabetical order erases everything, banishes every origin. Perhaps in places, certain fragments seem to follow one another by some affinity; but the important thing is that these little networks not be connected, that they do not slide into a single enormous network which would be the structure of the book, its meaning. It is in order to halt, to deflect, to divide this descent of discourse toward a destiny of the subject, that at certain moments the alphabet calls you to order (to disorder) and says: Cut! Resume the story in another way.

—Roland Barthes, from *Roland Barthes*, 1994

ambition

My best friend's nine-year-old cousin can't decide whether she wants to be an astronaut or Prime Minister. When I was young, I used to want to be either beautiful or a farmer's wife. I couldn't be both because if I was beautiful, then there was no way I would settle for just a farmer. I would be good enough for my very own sugar daddy. I knew what a sugar daddy was before I had heard of an engineer or a chartered surveyor.

♥ *See also Attitude; Bosses; Colin; Firefighting; Promotion;*
   Ultimatum

ants

I was sitting in the park during my lunch hour when an ant crawled over my leg. I squashed it with my thumb and flicked off its body with my fingers. Then I carried on eating my sandwiches.

Ants have not always left me so cold. I must have been about eleven when I found an ant colony in our garden. You have never seen anything so marvelous. It was like watching algebra in action. The worker ants walked in straight lines everywhere and seemed to know exactly where they were going.

But then I remembered something I'd learned at school and drew a line with my black felt-tip right across their path. It threw them into confusion. They wouldn't cross it even though it was just a drawing.

I told my father this at lunchtime. He said that we should respect ants for their innate civilization. They even milk aphids, he said, in the same way we milk cows. He went on and on about how clever ants were in a way he never talked about me.

After lunch, I boiled a kettle and poured the hot water over the colony. I sat there and watched the ants die. My eyes hurt from squeezing them together to make the tears come.

At supper, neither my father nor I said anything to each other. I was worried he might ask me what had happened to the ants.

❤ *See also Dogs; Engagement Ring; Jealousy; Outcast; Revenge; Tornadoes*

attitude

I work as a secretary in the media. The company I work for specializes in writing and producing technical newsletters for small- to medium-sized industrial businesses. Working in the media is something I don't always talk about because some people seem to think I'm showing off. This is something I would never do, but it's hard when all everybody wants to know is what it's like to have such an exciting job. Maybe this is why people in the media tend to stick together. But then again, the strange thing I have noticed is that when they're together, the only thing they talk about is what they are *going* to do and not what they *do* do. It seems they are all just filling in time before they become writers or film directors or actors or painters. It makes me feel dull for enjoying my job because there is absolutely nothing else I can imagine myself doing.

❤ *See also Dreams; Imposter Syndrome; Wobbling*

B

baked beans

My grandmother on my mother's side was a young girl in Liverpool during World War II. She can still remember the night the Heinz factory was bombed and how for days afterward the city smelled of cooked baked beans. It made the people in the city even hungrier than they were already.

Her mother—my great-grandmother—once spotted an unexploded bomb caught in a tree near their house. For hours she ran round getting people out of their houses and down to the shelter, where my grandmother was hiding. My great-grandmother wheeled the sick down, helped mothers with little children, and reassured the elderly.

She must have saved many, many lives that night, so I

can't blame my grandmother for still being annoyed, years later, that they didn't give her mother a medal for her bravery. Instead, they gave it to the lady who was in charge of making tea.

♥ *See also God; Mystery Tours; Noddy*

best friends

*A*t the age of twenty-five, my best friend, Sally, has become the mistress of a millionaire called Colin. This is not something that normally happens in our town. Just in films. She has given up her job, her nights out with the girls, and living in her studio flat. Because Colin has set her up in a flat near his office, she has taken a lodger to pay the mortgage on her own flat. And all this without a backward glance.

Recently, she spent five hours trying to find a dressmaker who was prepared to pick her jeans apart by hand and resew them so the tight seams would make no marks on her skin when Colin pulled them down.

We are no longer such good friends. She says she can't bear the way I look at her these days.

♥ *See also Danger; Friends; Influences; Ultimatum; Yields; Zzzz*

blackbirds, robins, and nightingales

Sometimes it is hard to distinguish between how you sound in your head and how other people seem to hear you.

For instance, I have noticed that I can make what I think is a perfectly pleasant comment but that it can still cause offense. I do not mean to have a sharp tongue, it is just the way the words come out.

Perhaps it is because I have such low self-esteem and do not think so much of myself as someone like Sally, for example.

Personally, though, I blame the nuns. At the convent school I went to, we were split into three groups for singing. There were the Nightingales, who could sing beautifully; the Blackbirds were all right; and the Robins were what Mother Superior called "orally challenged." I was one of only three Robins in the whole school, although I had a cold at the auditions, so it wasn't really fair.

The Robins were hardly ever allowed to sing in public and particularly not if the song had anything to do with God. We had to mouth along instead, which got very boring, and sometimes it was hard to keep in the words. Once, an unidentified Robin joined in on a particularly loud and lively hymn, one we all loved. In the middle of our Lord stamping out the harvest, Mother Superior held out her hand for silence.

"Hark!" she said, raising her other hand to her ear. "I can hear a Robin singing." Everyone looked at me.

That moment has always stayed with me. One of the things I hate most about myself is the way I blush in public even when I am not necessarily to blame. It is the same feeling that makes you itch every time anyone talks about fleas.

♥ *See also Captains; God; Outcast; Voices*

blood

*I*t used to be a craze at school to scratch the initials of your boyfriend into your arm with a compass and squeeze the skin until the blood came up. Then you'd rub ink over the graze so you'd be tattooed for life. Luckily, it rarely worked.

Once I was doing it with Sally, but as neither of us had a boyfriend at that time, we just dug the compass randomly into each other's arms. It made me think of the time I punctured my aunt's favorite leather sofa one Christmas with the screwdriver from the toy carpentry set I'd got from Santa. I did that again and again too.

It was Sally's idea to mix the blood drops together. She kept flicking her cigarette lighter, and we sang "Kumbaya" as we did it to make it seem more meaningful. Sally said that we were sisters now and that nothing could separate us, not even a boy.

♥ *See also Codes; Mars Bars; Vendetta; Yields; Zzzz*

bosses

The only trouble with my job is the bosses. My current one is possibly the worst I have ever had. His name is Brian. He is from Yorkshire and has a short bristly beard, which he is always fondling, and if I don't manage to look away, I can sometimes see his little tongue hanging out, all red and glistening.

Brian won't leave me alone. He seems to think we have a special relationship. He's always telling me that I mustn't mind if he teases me, that he does it to everyone he's fond of. "It means you're one of the family, Ver," he says, putting his arm round me.

It's funny, though, that while Brian is always standing too close to me, when it comes to work, he likes to dictate his typing for me into a machine rather than face-to-face. He'll do it even when I'm in the room, and he'll leave little messages to me as he's dictating, which means I have to hear them twice. Once he said into the machine: "Good morning, Verity. You're looking very nice this morning," so I called across, "Thank you, Brian," and he told me off for spoiling his dictation. He said he'd have to start again now. I left the room, and when I eventually listened to his tape, I noticed that this time he didn't say I looked nice.

Another time he dictated a rude joke to me. A man in an office asked to borrow another man's Dictaphone. The other man said no, he couldn't. He should use his finger to dial like everyone else.

I listened to this through my headphones with a stony

face because I knew Brian was watching me, hoping I would laugh.

♥ *See also Ambition; Zero*

boxing

I didn't tell Brian that Sally and I had started going to a Boxercise class at the local sports center. It would have only turned him on.

I wasn't very good at first. The instructor was American, a big man with a ponytail he was too old for. He followed me over to the punching bag and shouted out loudly that I was too much of a girl to box. He said it was because I was English and had been brought up to be polite. "Who would you like that punching bag to be?" he asked. "Who really pisses you off?" I couldn't think of anyone. I wouldn't really want to hurt Brian, even. Anyway, I told the instructor that I was half Irish. On my mother's side. He said that in that case, I definitely had to hit it harder. Harder, harder, harder. Eventually, I swung at it so hard that I kept on spinning even though I'd thrown my punch. The instructor clapped me on the back then and called me champ. He even started to sing "When Irish Eyes Are Smiling."

Sally and I couldn't stop laughing afterward. When we went for a drink, I noticed that we didn't hang back at the bar as we sometimes do. We made sure we got served straightaway, and then we took the best seats in the pub. When a man came to talk to us, Sally didn't flirt and throw her hair over her shoulder. She told him directly to go away. That she wanted to talk to her friend.

"You gave it hell, Verity," she kept saying, toasting me with her beer. "You gave it hell."

The next day, I walked sharper, straighter. As if I weren't a girl at all.

❤ *See also Gossip; Lesbians; Mustache; Weight*

breasts

Last week I was on my way home from work, walking past the wine bar, when a handsome Australian stopped me. He was dressed in a business suit, aged about thirty, very tanned, broad. He asked whether I'd have a drink with him. He said he was in town for only a couple of days, didn't know the area well, and was lonely. I weighed my options—drinks and a few laughs with him versus a microwaved meal in front of *EastEnders*.

When he ordered the bottle of wine, however, he asked for three glasses. Then his friend joined us. He was Australian too, but not tanned, not broad, aged around fifty. I didn't know you could get boring Aussies with glasses, hairy ears, and skinny bodies, but you can.

They talked together a lot of the time about intercomputer networking, HTML, broadband versus Bluetooth, although every so often, Peter, the young one, would look at me and wink. I suppose he meant to include me, but I was beginning to wonder why I was there. Then Peter went to the toilet, and after we'd sat there in silence for a bit, the other man leaned across the table and asked me how much. His breath smelled of pear drops, I remember, and all the time I was thinking, *How much what? How much wine? How much time?*

And then I realized.

I was running down the street, my face red, when Peter caught up with me. He grabbed my arm. I was shouting, "No, no," but weakly, so he turned me toward him and we kissed then. You know how sometimes when you kiss someone, your tongues intertwine and it feels like an electric shock racing through your body? As if your kiss has connected two wires between you, but all the resulting fizzles, crackles, and sparks are going on between your legs, not in your mouth? That's what happened then. That's why I agreed to go back to his hotel with him.

He touched my breasts a lot.

It is something I am sensitive about. You see, my breasts are very big. People can sometimes be cruel and shout out things about them in the streets. I hated them when I was growing up. I used to wear a too-tight swimsuit under my clothes to hold them down so no one would notice them. It used to make going to the toilet exhausting because I'd have to take off everything. Plus, at school we used to have these very short stall doors in the ladies' room, so I had to hold up all my clothes at waist height with one hand so no one could see.

Of course, I wasn't a virgin when I made love to Peter, but it was the first time anyone had touched my breasts like that. As if they weren't dirty, weren't something to be ashamed about. It seemed to mean something.

We had breakfast together in the morning, and he kissed me good-bye. There in the restaurant, like we were a proper married couple or something.

When I got into work, I didn't tell anyone. People kept saying how quiet I was. I went to the loo after a bit, and when I pulled down my knickers, I could smell Peter. That's when I started to cry.

I haven't heard from him since. It was my first time with a stranger like that. I hope it will be my last. I thought Colin was going to be a one-night stand for Sally at first. I get angry with Sally sometimes because she doesn't seem to feel the same guilt I felt about Peter.

💜 *See also Colin; True Romance*

captains

This is how Sally and I first became friends.

Like the singing, in my head I am completely co-ordinated as far as sports are concerned. Now that I am an adult, I don't have to do anything I don't want to, but I still like to lie in bed imagining how I can catch ball after ball in hands that open and caress rather than sting painfully. I picture my legs finding such a sweet rhythm as I run the 800-meter that I almost levitate off the ground, able to go on and on and on as I race past all the other runners.

In reality, I became the school expert at the rain dance I created in the hope that games would be canceled. It wasn't just the humiliation; it was the way your legs would get so cold on the hockey field, the skin red and blue and sharp with pain.

Sally walked in on me once in the girls' locker room just as I was jumping up and down in the deserted showers, hands on top of my head, elbows flapping. I was chanting, "Whoa, whoa, whoa, rain, rain, rain."

She took one look and left. I thought she might have been smiling, but I'd been too embarrassed to look closely. Neither of us said anything.

An hour later, we were standing at the edge of the sports field in the perfect sunshine. Sally was at the front of the class with the gym teacher, as she was always one of the team captains. I was standing at the back of the group of girls so I wouldn't have to keep getting out of the way when the other, more popular students were picked for the teams.

I thought it was a joke when Sally chose me before anyone else. I didn't want to go up at first, but everyone kept prodding me. Sally always picked me first after that.

I never asked her why, even afterward when we took a vow to tell each other everything. I always hoped it was because Sally was the one person who could look into my head and see those sweet catches I made in my dreams. How perfect everything was there.

♥ *See also Blackbirds, Robins, and Nightingales; Kindness; Vendetta; X-ray Vision*

codes

S all yan dI u se dt owrit eletter si ncod ebu twhe nyo utak ei ta sseriousl ya stha tyo uhav et ohav esomethin gt osa y. N othin gi swors etha ngoin gt oth etroubl eo funcoverin ga s ecre tan dfindin gnothin gther e. T hat' swhe nw estarte dshopliftin g. W e' dwrit elist so fwha twe' dtake ni nou rcod e. I t hin ktha twa swh yw ewer eneve rcaugh t. I fpeopl ecan' tunderstan dyo u, t he yten dt omak eyo uinvisibl e. T he ydon' tbothe rwit hyo u.

💜 *See also Friends; Indecent Exposure; Woolworths; Yields; Zzzz*

colin

I am starting to get suspicious about Colin. Maybe it's a hangover after my escapade with Peter, but I worry about the way he seems to treat Sally so casually.

Sally says that as long as he pays the bills and keeps her happy, she doesn't mind if he is a mad axman. She says his attitude is a relief.

"I'm blossoming," she says, and so she is.

I try to be happy for her, but when I walk up and down the road where Sally says Colin lives with his wife and family, I see no sign of him. I can't smell Colin in the air. Also, he is spending more and more time with Sally in what she calls their "love nest."

"Isn't his wife jealous?" I ask.

"If Colin doesn't mind, who cares?" Sally says, and

I must admit it seems a little bit odd that it's me who does.

♥ *See also Best Friends; Foreheads; Love Calculators; Stalking; Youth*

crème caramel

Sally has a friend who can devour a whole crème caramel from a plate in one go. I have seen her do it. She stands over the table with her hands behind her back, and then she sucks it up all at once without leaving a drop either on the plate or around her lips.

Sally herself can fit thirty-eight Maltesers into her mouth at once. She has to stuff them under her lips and in the spaces at the back of her jaw. It is not a very attractive sight, especially when she has to spit them all out again. But then neither is the crème-caramel-sucking-up trick, but at parties, people always ask to see them. It makes Sally and her friend the center of attention and the rest of us feel jealous.

Unfortunately, I don't like either Maltesers or crème caramel, and the one trick I do know is very complicated, involving three packs of cards. Could this be where I am going wrong?

♥ *See also Captains; Underwear; Wobbling*

D

daisies

My mother told me once that I was not sweet enough to be called after a flower. Something useful, yes, but not a flower. Her name was Rose, and I thought if I also had a pretty name, then I'd look more like her.

I called myself Daisy in secret and would talk about myself in the third person. "Daisy's nearly ready for bed now" or "Look how pretty Daisy looks in the mirror." It made me feel like I belonged. But then one day I blurted out something about wanting to be called Daisy, and everyone laughed.

"It sounds more like a cow," said my father, and he smiled fondly at my mother.

♥ *See also Ants; Names; True Romance; Zest*

danger

Sally will always be my only real friend, although I hope she never finds that out. She would probably think it was funny.

When we were growing up, our families were very different. Her parents used to go to the pub and drink sweet liqueurs that made her mother giggle. They were also what my parents called "Sunday drivers," which meant they went on outings. If I was lucky, they'd take me with them sometimes. Sally's mother called us "the girls," which I liked because it made me seem like a second daughter. As if Sally and I were interchangeable.

Once, we all went to a fete in the country and watched a local girl being crowned the Rose Queen. She sat giggling on a throne, holding a bunch of roses and surrounded by Rose Princes. These princes were all spotty and fat. The dishy boys were too busy throwing grass over the Rose Princesses to look at the Queen. The minute they'd put the crown on her, she'd become too much for them, although we couldn't see why she'd been picked in the first place.

Sally and I soon got bored because no one was throwing grass over us, so we went to look round. We found a bridge that was very crowded, so we joined the throng going over it. When we reached the middle, we suddenly heard the cracking and splitting of wood, and the bridge gave way.

Later, the man who owned the house and gardens came out and said that the trouble was that the bridge didn't lead anywhere, just to a shut gate; so what had happened was that people were coming straight back at the same time as others were crossing, and that meant there was too much weight in the middle for the bridge to hold. Considering the danger we'd all come through, he was surprisingly unsympathetic. It was the last time he was holding the fete on his grounds, he said, because he didn't understand why the public were all so keen to go over a bridge that went nowhere. And now he'd have to have the bridge mended, which was going to cost money he didn't have.

I read about an experiment that made men go over a very dangerous bridge, and when they got to the other side, they were shown photographs of women. All the men found the women more attractive than they would have done if they had not just had such an exciting experience. However, Sally and I both agreed that when the Rose Queen came to wish us well in the Red Cross tent, she was so ugly, we still wondered why she had been crowned.

Sally has always taken me places, shown me the way to behave, what to do. Sometimes I wonder if this is why she likes me. Sometimes I wonder if where she takes me is always the best place to go.

♥ *See also Best Friends; Worst-Case Scenario*

dogs

The chairman of our company has a Dalmatian dog called Jupiter. When he brings it into work, we have to take turns walking it at lunchtime. He seems to think it is a treat for us and makes jokes about how many girlfriends his dog has. It does make you wonder what he thinks we are.

Susan, the receptionist, once told me that she had taken a call from his French au pair. This girl was in tears because she had broken the vacuum cleaner when she was outside, Hoovering the lawn. Susan told her to take the vacuum cleaner inside and pretend it had never happened, but the girl kept crying, saying how much trouble she'd get into if the chairman's wife came back and found anything left on the grass.

Perhaps the wife was getting her revenge. You are always hearing stories about au pairs getting it on with their bosses. The chairman is good-looking enough. I have often smiled at him on the stairs or when we meet in the office, but I'm not sure he even notices me. He always calls me Veronica and laughs in this coughing little way when he sees me.

I remember reading that a jilted girlfriend once got back at her boyfriend by letting herself into his flat when he was away and planting grass seed all over the carpet. She went in every morning while he was on holiday and watered it. I would have loved to have seen his face when he opened the door.

We never had a dog, although I wanted one. I used to imagine waking up nearly every morning and hearing one barking for me downstairs. Once, I picked a particularly beautiful leaf and kept it in a glass bowl as a pet until I got bored of it. I do realize how pathetic this may sound now, but at the time I really loved that leaf.

♥ *See also Ambition; Revenge; Tornadoes*

doors

*I*t is impossible to have an advertisement in Britain that features a shut door. This is because so many people were locked in their bedrooms as children that even as adults, they automatically start to panic when a door isn't open. Even just an inch.

There were times when my mother used to tell me to stay in my bedroom. It wasn't cruel, she just wanted a break from looking after me. I'd have as many books as I wanted, treats to eat. I'd make myself a nest up there.

I always came down when my father came home, though. I was so happy to see him, but he'd be tired after his day at work. He said he just wanted to spend some quiet time with my mother. I had so much to talk about, after my day of reading, but he didn't seem to want to hear it.

❧ *See also Houses; Noddy; Property; Velvet; Yellow*

dreams

*S*ally once went out with a man who liked to record her dreams in a diary. She had to break it off with him because she got too exhausted. She'd be awake all night trying to think of interesting things for him to write about.

❧ *See also Codes; Mistaken Identity; Utopia*

E

ears

I like to stick cotton swabs in my ear and turn them round, pushing harder and harder. I crave the satisfaction it brings. Sometimes when friends are over, all I can think of is that round plastic jar of swabs until I have to go into my bedroom and clean my ears. It's like an itch. Once I twisted too hard, and my head filled with a howling pain. I vowed then never to do it again, until the next time.

There was a boy at school called Stewart Griffiths. One day he was swinging on his chair during geography when the teacher called him to attention. Stewart was startled, lost his balance, and as he fell backward onto the floor, the pencil he was holding at his ear pierced right through his eardrum. He screamed.

Three years later, when I started attending that school and joined that class, the other children were still talking about the loudness of that scream. When we were fifteen, I went out with Stewart Griffiths and felt the reflected glory from his fame. He would still scream on the playground for money.

The trouble was that Stewart was boring when he wasn't making a noise. He wanted to be a lorry driver, and sometimes when we were lying together on his bed, he'd be able to name the type of lorry that went past the window just from the sound of its tires. He seemed to feel that this was particularly clever as he was still deaf in one ear from the pencil incident.

❤ *See also Captains; the Fens; Sounds*

elephant's egg

We went to London Zoo for my eighth birthday, and I fell in love with the elephants. I wanted to move in with them and be the little elephant that never strayed from her mother's side. I wanted people to say how sweet I was, and take pictures of me, and have my father wrap his trunk around me, swishing the flies off or sprinkling water over me to wash my back.

The next year, the day before my birthday, I asked to go and see the elephants again. My mother said once was enough, but when I got back from school that afternoon, there was a message from the zoo. Apparently, the elephant at London Zoo had laid an egg especially for me and my family to eat. It was going to come on my birthday.

The only trouble was that the zookeeper left it on our doorstep during the only two minutes in the day that I stopped watching for him. I took it into the kitchen, where my mother was waiting to cook it. She was cross with me for not keeping a proper lookout because it meant she wasn't able to thank the keeper for bringing it all that way.

This happened every year until I was thirteen. I never managed to catch the zookeeper. My mother never managed to thank him.

An elephant's egg is not like an ordinary egg. The

white tastes like mashed potato, and the yolk is never runny, being a bit like a large round sausage. I've had sausage and mashed potatoes many times since, but never anything as good as those elephant's eggs.

❤ *See also The Queen; The Queen II*

endings

*E*ver since the Australian incident, I have been spending more time in my flat. My best treat is to pop into a bookshop and pick up a book to read. Then I curl up on the sofa with a bottle of wine and read myself into a trance.

The sort of books I like best are those in which I can completely lose myself. At first, you sit with the unopened book on your lap waiting to meet the main character with that sense of anticipation you get on blind dates. Is this person going to be your new best friend? And then there's a moment—normally, just over halfway through—when your heart grows until it's too big for your body because all these dreadful things are happening in the book and there's nothing you can do to stop them. You can't even tell the characters they're making all the wrong decisions. You've just got to keep on reading. But then you get to the last words, and you can't believe it—you keep your fingers on the end sentence because it can't all finish there. It's as if they've shut the door and left you on the other side, unwanted. And you cared so much. And there's no way to make them see how much you cared.

A teacher at school told us that fairy stories always end

with the prince and princess living happily ever after because what the writers were really saying, but couldn't, was
that they would die eventually. Apparently, it's a way of
helping children to understand life and death. It was rain-
ing when he was telling us this. I'll never forget the sound of
the rain falling on the flat roof of the classroom. Somehow
it always rained when he read us stories that year.

Anyway, what he told us, very sternly, was that no one
could expect to live happily ever after. It just didn't happen. There are no happy endings, he said.

♥ *See also Breasts; Stepmothers; True Romance; Yellow; Zzzz*

engagement ring

Colin has given Sally a ring. It isn't an engagement
ring, but that's the finger she wears it on even though
I tell her it's bad luck.

She won't let me try it on or even touch it. She says she
remembers me telling her about how I posted my mother's
engagement ring in my piggy bank when I was six.

It's true my mother cried in secret for days after the
ring first went missing. She didn't tell anyone. That was
the strange thing. She didn't even tell my father. I'm sure
about this because I think if she had, he'd have started
one of those inquisitions he was so fond of. Instead, she
was quieter than normal. I'd come across her in odd
rooms, frantically searching through cupboards, drawers,
pockets, piles of things. Sometimes her eyes looked white
and strained, as if she was forcing herself not to weep.

Sally still can't understand why I never told my mother

what I had done, but it was one of those china piggy banks you had to break to open, and I loved the spotty smoothness of my pig. And then, of course, it was too late. I wouldn't have been able to put the ring back on the dressing table and pretend it hadn't happened because Mum had moved the table to the other side of the room. I guess now she'd been taking up the carpet to check that the ring hadn't fallen down there.

Dad went mad when he found my mother had lost her ring, but it was such a long time afterward that I couldn't feel guilty anymore. If my mother had really cared she'd have made a fuss at the time. She was always losing things.

❤ *See also Daisies; Mistaken Identity; True Romance; Voices*

$\mathcal{F}$

fashion

My favorite book when I was growing up was *The Little White Horse*. There were two things about it I remember particularly. One was the sugary biscuits that were left in a silver tin in the heroine's tower bedroom. Some even had little pastel flowers iced on them. The other was the heroine's journey to the castle to stay with her unknown uncle. She was nervous but still able to get pleasure from her beautiful laced-up boots tucked away under her long skirts. Even though no one else could see them, she knew they were there and that was enough. It gave me a thrill of recognition.

It probably shaped my life. Made me see the strength you could get from having the right kind of secrets.

I spend a lot of time shopping. I search out clothes that have special things about them that only I will know. I hug these to me: a particular color that makes you want to eat it; a lining of soft plum silk; the Liberty-print trim to a denim pocket; a perfectly shaped pleat that kicks up the edge of a skirt.

Coco Chanel knew all about this. She used to sew a gold chain invisibly into the hems of her jackets so they would be ideally weighted around the bottom.

I think if I could have a jacket like that, I would die happy. I'd be buried in it.

❤ *See also Codes; Start-rite Sandals; Underwear; Women's Laughter*

fat women

I am the last person to judge anyone else based on appearances alone, but have you noticed how difficult it is to see a fat woman and a small, thin man together and not think of them having violent, needy, and possibly perverted sex?

❤ *See also Indecent Exposure; Sex; Toys; Voyeur; Weight; Wrists*

the fens

Every time I tell people I come from the Fens, the only thing they can think to say is "Well, there's certainly a lot of sky there." If this is the first thing you think of, here are three things you might not know about the Fens:

1. A lot of the children I went to school with had webbed feet. In the Fens, this is quite usual. They weren't heavy like duck feet, but just a sliver of thin skin, so transparent as to be like silver, between each toe. When these children flexed their toes, it was the most beautiful sight you could imagine, especially after swimming, when the drops of water would glisten and sparkle.

2. The roads in the Fens are long and straight and run alongside treacherous dikes. They look even straighter because the houses on either side are slipping lower and lower back into the soil. If you are quiet, you can almost hear it sucking at you. Anyway, because it gets so dark at night—all that sky—a lot of people have accidents and drive into the ditches and die. Often when you are driving in the Fens during the daylight, you see bouquets of flowers by the side of the road for the tragedy of the night before.

At the bank opposite our house, a doctor had a terrible accident with his wife. He managed to get out of the car before it got submerged, but she drowned. He was so grief-stricken that he sat on the side of the road until he was sure she had died. It became a craze for many months afterward, imagining just what it must have felt like with all that water pressing against the car window and being able to see your husband through the waves, watching you scream.

3. Not many people appreciate that if you lie in a field of broad-bean plants in flower, just as the sun is going down, you will find yourself surrounded by the smell of Chanel No. 5. It just goes to show that if you know where to look, there is beauty in even the most unlikely places.

💜 *See also Fat Women*

firefighting

Sometimes when I'm busy at work, I think of Sally's new life and wonder how she is keeping herself occupied. When we left school and started work, we had so many plans. We were going to start a business together, and although we could never decide what to do, we had lots of ideas. We were going to train in martial arts and hire ourselves out as bodyguards. We'd look like classy dates, but if someone tried to kill our partners, we'd be able to high-kick our way out of trouble. We were going to run a truly caring furniture removal company, make novelty cushions, revamp people's wardrobes. In the meantime, I went to work for a bank and Sally got a job selling advertising space for the local newspaper. That's when she persuaded me to follow her into the media, although I was worried at first because my personality has never been as bouncy as hers. I could never cold-call like Sally could.

For example, one summer holiday Sally got us both a job selling fire extinguishers. We were supposed to walk into shops, and while one of us distracted the shop assistant, the other would start a small fire that we would then put out with the fire extinguisher to show how efficient it was.

My father found out what we had to do on the day we were due to start, and he banned me from joining Sally on safety grounds. Although she kept telling me what fun she was having and how much I was missing, I was secretly relieved. Sometimes the things Sally makes herself do frighten me.

❤ *See also Attitude; Danger; Imposter Syndrome; Sex*

foreheads

Sally asked me what I thought of Colin.

I said he was okay. Nothing special. Not worth throwing your life away. But then Sally said that Colin had told her I was a bit intense. Apparently, I keep staring at him.

At first, I didn't know what he was talking about. But then I realized. Colin plays rugby. He'd come to the pub with a group of his friends after they'd been playing in the park. It's true, I couldn't stop looking at them. They all had the same foreheads. A bulging shelf that hung over their eyes and made them look unfocused and brainless.

Other men didn't have this. They even shared the same wavy wrinkles across their foreheads. It was as if an empty space had been badly filled with cement, and then someone had made patterns on it with a comb when it was still wet.

I wanted to ask why rugby players look and sound permanently concussed, but they were all too busy talking to one another and ignoring Sally and me. I didn't think Colin had seen me looking.

❤ *See also Nostrils; Vendetta; X-rated; Youth*

friends

Every time I go out now with the girls, we talk about Sally.

I think that nowadays we spend more time thinking about her than we ever did when she was spending time with us. We wonder if she's really happy, if she thinks Colin is genuine in his desire for her, what it must be like to have such a one-sided relationship. We agree we only have her best interests at heart.

We are supportive, even though Sally doesn't always deserve it. I know that Miranda hasn't forgotten the time we were talking about making love and she was explaining the importance of truly caring for the other person and treating yourself as if you were someone precious.

"I could never have inappropriate, meaningless sex," Miranda said. She was so earnest that Sally was the only one round the table who didn't nod.

"I could," she said, staring at the businessman at the next table and ignoring Miranda's frown. She left the restaurant with the businessman, and afterward, she wouldn't tell anyone what happened. Not even when we begged. She said we wouldn't approve.

It was so typical of her, but even so, the last thing we all want is for Sally's relationship not to work out.

Whenever I ring Sally to pass on everyone's best wishes, she laughs.

"We're here waiting for you if things don't work out," I tell her, and she says that's just what she's worried about.

♥ *See also Outcast; Vendetta*

G

glenda g-spot

I told Monica at work that I don't go out very much in the evening, so she invited me around to her house. I thought it was just going to be the two of us, but when I got there, I found she was having a sex party.

This is like Tupperware for desperate women, although we didn't do "it"; in fact, not much of the evening was about actually doing "it." There were just lots and lots of gadgets for sale that simulated doing "it." There were about ten women there, all older than me. Monica's age. We sat in a circle and passed these gadgets round, sometimes without saying a word. Every so often, Monica walked round with a tray of little biscuits smeared with hummus and pâté and filled up our glasses with fizzy sweet wine.

The woman who was organizing the party was like a perverted Mary Poppins. Just when you thought it was all finished, she'd put her hand into an enormous canvas bag and pull out something else. She made us play games and gave us all silly names. I was "Glenda G-spot," Monica was "Wendy Wet-dream," and the girl sitting next to me was "Cathy Come." It was hard to know whether to call one another by our real names or the names on the labels the woman stuck on our chests.

Cathy Come and I got into the final round of one game where we had to pass an enormous black dildo under our chins between each other without dropping it. Cathy Come cheated because she kept angling it, so it was difficult to get hold of. Mind you, I was quite pleased to come in second because Cathy won the dildo but I got a bottle of an apricot-flavored sauce, which seemed nicer somehow.

I left when the woman drew a blow-up man out of her bag. One of his legs was stapled up from when a dog had got hold of it, she said. The air kept fizzling out of him, and I don't like to say where the nozzle was to blow into.

♥ *See also Liqueur Chocolates; Names; Toys*

glitter

It worries me that all everyone thinks about these days is sex. I asked Sally about this the other day, and she told me a story about a friend of hers who is a nurse. This friend's elderly mother came to stay the night before she was due to have a gynecological examination in the hospital Sally's friend works in. The mother was very nervous, so she spent a lot of time preparing in Sally's friend's bathroom before her appointment. She wanted to be very clean because no man had looked at her "down there" before, not even her own husband.

The examination went very well, but just as he was finishing, the doctor said: "I would like to thank you for making such a big effort."

Sally's friend and her mother discussed this afterward. Could it just be because Sally's friend's mother was so clean? Eventually, they went to the bathroom and looked through the cabinet to see the lotions the mother had used.

Imagine Sally's friend's horror when she realized her mother had sprayed her pubic hair with green glitter spray for the doctor. At work the next day, everyone was laughing about her mother's private parts and how when her legs were wide open, they were lit up like a Christmas tree.

Sally and I laughed about it too, although I stopped after a while.

"Why did your friend have glitter in her bathroom, anyway?" I asked, but Sally says I'm too literal.

Now I can't stop wondering if she sprays herself with glitter for Colin.

❤ *See also Indecent Exposure; Sex*

g o d

I used to spend a great deal of time listening for messages from God. Despite what the nuns said, I thought that I had a vocation and that if I didn't concentrate, I might miss the sign. In the same way, I used to check my hands for stigmata every morning.

I never got a message. I know now this was a blessing. Imagine if you did spot the star of Bethlehem one night on your way back from a club? Could you really tell anyone without being locked up? Or what if your sign was so stupid, it made people laugh? Like that Victorian couple who also gave up a lot of their lives to listening out for God. When the message finally came, they were beside themselves with excitement. They probably told all their friends, so imagine their humiliation when they eventually deciphered it.

"Eat more slowly," God told them.

❤ *See also Ambition; Codes; Phantom E-mails*

gossip

Every time Brian finds me talking to someone at work, he tells me off for being a gossip. But why is it that two men found talking together are discussing something important whereas two women are always gossiping?

♥ *See also Boxing; Glitter; Mustache; Women's Laughter*

grief

There was a little boy in the park the other day. He was dressed in the full England kit, like a miniature footballer. He even had those long socks on, and when he ran, he did that sideways swagger at the hips men do to make it look as if they aren't properly running. Just getting to somewhere quickly.

But then he fell over, and his face went all square. Not just the shape of his face, but every little feature in it went square. His mouth was the most obvious. It turned into a letterbox in the middle of this red block. Even his eyes looked like small, angular black stamps. His whole body went rigid too, and when his shoulders shook, they turned into straight lines that went up and down, up and down, like a lift. I watched as his mother ran up and tried to get hold of him. It was difficult for her at first because his edges were too sharp, but then he suddenly deflated into a rag doll, and she picked him up and took him over to the bench and made him happy again.

Just like that. I saw how she made him happy. One second he was crying, and the next he was pointing at a dog and laughing.

I think the secret is in getting the tears out. Some mornings I wake up and I know I've been crying in my sleep, but I just can't get the tears out. That's when you think you're drowning. You're not sharp or square. Just an empty outline filled to the brim with lukewarm water that numbs everything inside you. You're too full to take anything in and too blocked to let anything out. That's grief. Everything else is just sadness, and seeing a funny dog can make you better.

❤ *See also Happiness; Illness; Why?; You*

gwyneth paltrow

*I*f I looked like Gwyneth Paltrow, nothing could possibly go wrong in my life. And that's all I want to say about her. Basically.

❤ *See also Breasts; Star Quality*

ℋ

hair

My hair is very long and black. There's a little nub of black at the end of each strand. Like a small pool of ink. I can squash it between two pieces of paper so it sticks and leaves a dark streak when you press on it. I can even write with it. Sometimes I find marks I have left in books and forgotten about. Once I even did it to a library book. If I am ever captured, I will be able to write a note with my hair. It is the one advantage brunettes have over blondes.

Actually, I have started to pull my hair out. Each time I tug at a strand, there is a second when I don't think I'm going to be able to bear the pain. It's the only thing I can think about, but it never lasts long enough. When it's over, I flick the hair to the ground and immediately pull at another.

I was trying on some clothes the other day, and I saw what I thought was a bald patch at the back of my head in the mirror. My legs nearly buckled, but when I went closer, I saw that it was just the reflection from the light shining on my hair. I told myself that I would stop. Not that day, but one day soon.

When I was at school, I played netball with a girl called Susan Armstrong. One day she was just standing on the court scratching her head and daydreaming. When the ball suddenly came toward her, she put her hands up in a panic to catch it, but she was still holding on to her hair, and she yanked out a whole handful. It never grew back. The skin underneath was tighter and shinier than her face. It was like looking at the moon.

She couldn't have minded because she used to show it to everyone. Mind you, she was a bit of an exhibitionist. When she left school, she went to work in a fish-and-chips shop and had to wear a little hat over her head. Maybe it was because she couldn't let us see her bald patch anymore that she would let us smell her arm. It was as if the oil and vinegar from all those fish suppers had soaked into her skin. I used to love smelling Susan's arm, but one day when there was no one else around, I couldn't stop myself from leaning forward and licking her. Not hard. My tongue didn't actually reach the flesh, it just brushed the hairs on her arm backward and forward. I could almost feel each grain of salt in my mouth.

Susan kept her arm still, and when I looked up into her face, I could swear I saw right through her eyes and into her soul. It was moonlike too, with patches waiting to be filled.

Even though she gave me extra chips at the shop that day, I never went back. I told everyone that I'd decided fish-and-chips weren't healthy.

💜 *See also Fashion; Lesbians; Visible*

happiness

There is a new campaign at work that has been designed to expand the horizons of the support staff. This means that instead of the weekly gossipy lunch, we now have speakers who come in to talk about our personal development.

I enjoy most of these.

One of the best has been a man who came in and told us how to be happy. He said something that has stuck with me. He asked us what we'd do if we went into a room that had two doors leading from it. One had a notice on it that read "Lecture on how to get to heaven," and the other read "Heaven." Which one would you go through?

We all thought about this, and more than half of us said that we'd go to the lecture first because it would make us better prepared. He laughed.

"Why not just go straight in?" he asked, and we couldn't tell him because then we would have had to admit that it was because we didn't feel quite up to heaven just at that moment. He was so confident. It was as if he'd been covered in shiny plastic that kept out all worries. Even his teeth looked as if they'd been carved from white rubber. You felt if you were to punch him, your fist would bounce right back and smack you one in the face. And you'd probably deserve it.

He told us that we had to write our obituaries. I tried all afternoon, but Brian kept leaning across and reading it out to everyone. Monica must have told him about the sex party, because he keeps calling me Glenda and winking. I think Brian is the kind of person who would read other people's diaries.

♥ *See also Grief; Imposter Syndrome; Kindness; Positive Thinking; Wobbling*

heroines

One of my heroines is Grace Darling, the lighthouse keeper's daughter. This is not only because she had trouble with her hair. In fact, she and I have much else in common, including growing up with unsupportive mothers.

I first developed a craze on Grace when we went on holiday to Bamburgh. Every time I walked along by the sea, I would see the lighthouse at Longstone where she lived. I used to secretly call her "my Grace," although she would never have played with me, of course.

No, I'll never forget visiting the Grace Darling Museum and hearing her story for the first time. It wasn't that she risked her life to save all those people that startled me; it was the similarities between us. For a long time, I wondered if she had been reincarnated in me, and I took to wearing a shawl over my clothes until my mother stole it one night and refused to give it back because she said I was making a fool of myself.

It was Grace who saw me through this crisis. I thought of how her mother had tried to force her to finish her breakfast when she wanted to go out to sea straightaway. And then to cap it all, her mother's last words to Grace before she left that day were: "Oh, Grace, if your father is lost, I'll blame a' you for this morning's work."

This didn't stop her mum from sharing in the glory when it came. She even got a jug sent to her by a well-wisher with the inscription FOR THE MOTHER OF GRACE DARLING. I would love it if my mother had received something like that. FOR VERITY BELL'S MOTHER.

In fact, my mother is just one of the reasons that I have never been able to carry out any heroic actions. That, plus no one ever needed saving during all the time we stayed at Bamburgh.

But, yes, I have always liked and empathized with strong women.

♥ *See also Boxing; Marathons; Voices; Weight*

horoscopes

The other day, I noticed a worrying thing. I have got in the habit of looking up Sally's horoscope before mine. It's a good thing I don't believe in them anyway, because I am a Taurus and we never seem to have much fun. Besides, Saturn is fighting Mars this week, and I need to watch my back at work. Someone will be hiding a deep secret from me. I didn't read Sally's properly, but I did notice that not everyone close to her will have her best interests at heart. She refuses to tell me what star sign Colin is born under, but I bet it's Sagittarius. I have never trusted Sagittarians. They are too popular.

♥ *See also Omens; Questions*

horror movies

*T*he only horror movie I have ever enjoyed was one that I went to with Sally. When we first started earning money, we'd go up to London to spend the day shopping and sometimes fit in an early film. One day, I wanted to go and see a rerun of *The Sound of Music* in Leicester Square, but somehow Sally got the wrong tickets and we ended up in the cinema next door.

Sally wouldn't let me leave straightaway, although she promised I could if I really, really hated the film, but I'd have to go home on my own. She also said she'd hold my hand if I got scared. The heroine was a beautiful female photographer who saw death through her camera lens. Eventually, the murderer she watched came after her in real life.

Something funny happened in the cinema that night. It was as if every one of us in the audience had been plugged into one another. The film can't have been that scary, but we all screamed as one, clung to complete strangers, and at the end, when the murderer was climbing up the stairs to kill the photographer, we all started shouting at her to "Turn around and get the gun" at the top of our voices. It was exhilarating. When the film finally ended, all of us were laughing in our seats, none of us seemed to have the energy to move, and the cinema bars were full with people who wanted to talk about what had just happened.

Sally and I giggled for the whole of the train journey home, and when I woke up the next morning, I knew that something wonderful had happened. I'd been part of something. I felt a deep sense of anticlimax for a long time afterward.

♥ *See also Danger; God; Sculpture; Why?*

houses

Most Saturdays, our family would go and look at smart houses in the area that were up for sale.

It was just a hobby, though, because we could never really afford any of the homes we looked at. When we saw one we particularly liked, we would spend the week afterward talking together about which piece of furniture would go where. We'd have arguments trying to decide what color we would paint each room, which would be my bedroom, where my mother would sit and read in the evenings.

Sometimes I'd watch my parents walk round someone else's house hand in hand, and I'd know what it was like to feel secure.

One house we saw was perfect. It started singing to us the minute we walked in. My mother and father opened cupboards in the large kitchen, sat on the window seat and watched where the sun fell, stood in silence looking at the view from the bedroom. I went downstairs to leave them in peace and found a room we hadn't gone into before.

It was extraordinary. Inside, every wall was covered in doors, all hung in identical white-painted doorframes. I opened one at random, and all that was behind it was the wallpaper. I opened another, and then another, but all I could find was nothingness. It took me a long time to find the right door, the door out, and by the time I did, I was crying.

No one spoke in the car on the way home, and when I followed my father inside, I watched him kick our kitchen table when he thought no one was looking. My parents were upset that they couldn't afford the house, but I was pleased. It took me a long time before I could open a door without a feeling of dread, but when I told my father about it, he wouldn't believe me.

♥ *See also Doors; Kitchen Equipment; Magazines; Property; True Romance; Yellow*

I

ice cream

When I was six, I was taken to see *The Railway Children* but had to leave halfway through because I put my ice cream down the neck of the woman sitting in front of me. The funny thing is that I still want to do the same every time I go to the movies. Just to see what will happen.

I used to like to bite off the end of my cone and suck the ice cream out that way. It upsets me nowadays to see that even advertisements for ice-cream products are using sex to make them appealing. I once gave up sex for a whole year. It was amazing how much extra time I had. It wasn't that I was doing it all the time. It was the side effects. If you're not interested in sex, then there's hardly a book, a film, a piece of music that you need to bother with. There are so many more hours in the day.

♥ *See also Glitter; Sex; Victim; Zero*

illness

I hate being ill.

Other people at work have what they call "duvet days," but I think they're probably the ones who have never come across really sick people. Otherwise, they wouldn't pretend.

When my mother was in hospital, my father and I used to go and visit her every day. We would take a picnic for after our visit and have it in the little garden by the side of the car park. It became important that every day we'd have the same things to eat. Cheese and ham sandwiches, apples, and to wash it down, we'd share a bottle of sparkling water.

My father would just sit there and cry silently. The tears would roll down his cheeks, and he'd not do anything to stop them. Sometimes people would look at us and then stare sympathetically at me, which confused me because Dad's tears were something you stopped noticing after a while.

I used to talk to Dad, not about emotions or anything. I stuck to facts. I'd tell him how many trees were in the garden. How much every separate item of our lunch had cost. I'd read out the football scores to him, right through to the third division. I'd go through the television guide, what was on each channel, even the digital ones that we didn't have. He'd nod away at me so he'd seem to be listening, but then he'd turn and say something like: "Your mum was so beautiful. I never knew what she saw in me. Even now, every time she goes out of the door, I think she won't bother to come back. She always seemed so precious. I was scared to touch her, you know. Scared I'd break her or something."

Then we'd go back up to the ward, and I'd look at Mum and try to see what he'd seen in her. We were never sure how much she took in, but the nurses said it was important to keep trying to stimulate her. I'd tell her some of the things I'd just told Dad, and he'd nod away again, as if I was right. As if he remembered. And then he'd touch her hand, and I saw that he still saw her as precious, was still worried he might lose her. She became whiter and whiter the longer she stayed in hospital, until she seemed to become part of the hospital bed. Her skin was as transparent and papery-dry as the sheet. Dad and I got browner, though, from all the picnic lunches we had in the sun. Then one day I looked at my parents' hands together, and it seemed Mum had already died. Her hand looked like a marble effigy next to his.

When Dad went into hospital not long afterward, it seemed like a cruel joke. Some of the nurses even remembered us. I sat in the garden on my own then, although Sally came with me a few times. She took me out for lunch once. We had chips, I remember, and my tears kept flowing. Just like Dad's.

Eventually, the waiter came over. "Is everything all right?" he asked. I guess he was worried I'd cause a scene or something.

Sally was wonderful. She looked him up and down, and then she said: "No. Everything is not all right. These chips have upset my friend very much. Can't you see how sad they have made her?"

We laughed then. It was the first time I'd laughed for about a year and I had been afraid I'd forgotten how to, but when we got back to the hospital, they told us Dad had passed away while we were out. He'd just given up the fight, they said. But I knew he'd died of a broken heart.

This is why I would never pretend to be ill to have a day off work.

♥ *See also True Romance*

imposter syndrome

There was another interesting speaker at work. She told us that we had to believe we were worthy of our positions in life, but that just made us laugh because she didn't seem to understand that most of us secretaries think the opposite—that we're actually much better than the position we've ended up in.

Still, she also said a lot of things that made sense. She said that many women have this arrow hanging over them. They think that at any minute, someone is going to walk over to them, whatever it is they're doing—even if (espe-

cially if) they're in the middle of something important—
and tell them that they've been found out. That they're not
good enough to continue. Please, could they leave the
room and let someone better carry on in their place.

My body felt electric. I couldn't believe other people
have this arrow too. It follows you around, pointing at
you in a crowd and telling you exactly what you are doing
wrong. Sooner or later, someone else is going to spot it
and realize exactly how useless you are. Probably when
your mouth is full of cheese sandwich and you can't defend yourself.

It was reassuring to learn that this is a common syndrome. I could tell the others felt relieved too. We were
more cheerful that afternoon than when we were writing
our obituaries, although I have noticed that these personal development sessions have encouraged us to talk
about our feelings more. I am not sure this is altogether a
good thing. What happens when it all goes wrong and
there's nowhere to hide?

❤ *See also Codes; Happiness; Teaching; Why?*

indecent exposure

It is a fact of life: in any town, even one as small as
this, men often expose themselves to you. I feel rather
like a nurse must feel about this. You see this little thing
curled up like a shrimp and the expectant male face above
it, waiting for you to react, and most of the time, it's not
remotely sexy or even frightening. Just a bit boring.

Sally has a number of set phrases designed to wither a man at fifty paces, but that seems rather unnecessary. We're all just trying our hardest to survive—admittedly, some more than others.

❤ *See also Boxing; Weight*

influences

My mother was a great one for lists. She even spoke in bullet points.

"And another thing," she'd say. Even when she was in full flow of one of her furies, she could tick off on her fingers all the points that made her angry.

The list she particularly loved was all the bad influences on me. My problem was that I was easily led by so many people and things:

1. Every English teacher I'd ever had. Especially Mr. Shepherd in year ten, who wanted to take me and Marian Riley on a camping holiday in his two-man tent after we'd been reading Thomas Hardy in class. We were going to go to Dorset and explore Hardy country, but my mother wouldn't let me go.

2. Suzanne Gibson. I never really understood this one. Suzanne lived in a hotel because her house had been repossessed when her father couldn't pay the bills anymore. I always lived in fear that my mother would publicly accuse Suzanne of being a bad influence on me, for then Suzanne might think I'd been telling people we were

friends when in fact she had never even bothered to look at me. She was far too glamorous.

3. The "Cathy and Claire" column in *Jackie* magazine. Mum had read it once and been shocked by the sex advice offered. She never knew I'd written to them, explaining how I'd fallen in love with a girl in the Lower Sixth. I got a letter back from them saying that it was just a crush and that I should join more sporting clubs to broaden my interests and make me a more rounded person.

4. Mr. and Mrs. Goodman, Sally's parents. They were always too jolly and family-oriented for my mother. Apparently, it was a sign of how vulgar they were. I hadn't realized until then that only common people are happy. It is posher as well as more interesting to be haunted by internal ghosts who make you miserable. Strangely, my mother liked Sally. She thought she'd come to a bad end and was therefore a good example for me of what not to do.

♥ *See also Danger; Telephone Boxes; Underwear; Zzzz*

jacuzzi

I have always liked the idea of meeting someone in a Jacuzzi. Of falling in love surrounded by shiny bubbles. Plus, when you've just swum yourself into a trance, you leave the rest of the world behind you. Relaxing after this is when I think you'd be able to talk about anything.

At our local swimming pool, they turn the overhead lights off after nine o'clock at night and start playing country music through the loudspeakers. All the kids have gone home and there're only adults left, plowing up and down the lengths, listening to words of love all around them and lit up from below the water so they look like gods.

♥ *See also Imposter Syndrome; Mistaken Identity*

jealousy

Why does Sally have to be given so much in life?

It doesn't really help her. She takes so much for granted. She complains about things as if she really doesn't care about them. She says she wants to live on her own and doesn't want to be beholden to anyone. She wants no possessions, no ties, no responsibilities. She says this is her ambition. But you can really leave things behind only if you have them in the first place—a family, a relationship, opinions. Otherwise, you're not even running away. You're merely existing somewhere, anywhere, else.

Still, the good thing is that I am not at all jealous of Sally. We each bring our own attributes to the relationship that are mutually beneficial. I am completely happy with my own life. I wish Sally well in hers.

Sally and I are friends. No, no, no. I am not jealous of Sally. I am especially not jealous of Sally's relationship with Colin.

💗 *See also Zzzz*

john

I can't wait to tell Sally.

The most amazing thing has happened.

I have fallen in love. I feel glowing. I feel fantastic. I have just walked down the street, and everybody smiled at me. Men whistled at me. I feel like a goddess. I look down at my arms, and my skin looks as if it has been sprinkled with diamond dust.

Everybody is so much nicer, funnier, prettier. And so am I.

His name is John.

K

k a t e

*J*ohn has a wife. Sally told me first. Well, she didn't know exactly, but what she said was: "If he e-mails you from work, he is married. If it is always him who has to call you, he has children. If he doesn't have any hobbies, it is because he has a family life, not no life."

I asked John about it but he was going to tell me anyway. Right after we talked about it, he asked me to tell him a joke, so I believe him when he says being married isn't a problem.

"Two parrots were on a perch," I said. "One said to the other 'Can you smell fish?'"

Sally told me this joke. It makes everyone laugh, but I don't really understand it. I think it might be surrealist. When I asked John if this was so, he told me that I was funny and that he loved me. He couldn't tell me why that should surprise him so.

John's wife's name is Kate. I don't like the way they're next to each other in the alphabet. My name is Verity, so I'm right at the end, out of the way.

He doesn't love her. He never has. They are together just for the sake of the children.

♥ *See also Women's Laughter*

kindness

I want to go round the world carrying out random acts of kindness. I want to buy extravagant foods and leave them on pensioners' doorsteps. I want to get up on a snowy day and wipe the windshields of every car in the street. I want to entertain small children so their mothers can sleep. I want to take every homeless person to the Ritz for a night. I want to hire the Bolshoi Ballet and put on performances in Trafalgar Square so commuters can be inspired on their way to work. I want to stand on street corners and wait for blind men to come along so I can lead them across the street. I want to tape the wings of injured birds with lollipops and Band-Aids. I want to distribute food to orphans, take guns off soldiers, rid the world of nuclear threats.

I want everyone to feel as happy as I do. I am so fucking happy, I think I'm going to explode.

♥ *See also Grief; Imposter Syndrome; Nostrils*

kisses

I've taught John to do that twiddly thing with his tongue that the Australian did. He should be in one of those kissing booths at village fetes. I am sure there are many, many people who would pay to be kissed like that.

The funny thing is, I sold my first kisses for money. My mother would slip me cash for kissing my grandmother whenever we went to visit her. I would have done it for free, but I pretended I didn't like touching her prickly, hairy, old-lady cheeks because it seemed to give my mother pleasure. In fact, I wanted to rub my skin against my grandmother's forever. She smelled of lavender and dried rosebuds and those thin tubes of Parma Violet sweets. Very different from my mother, who had a tinny, chemical smell that stung you when you got too close.

When my grandmother was small, she won a book for good attendance at her Sunday school. She kept it very carefully on a small pine shelf with the few books she had, and I was never allowed to look at any of them. For some reason, this shelf was in her bathroom.

One day when I was staying with her, I crept up to the bathroom and read it. It was called *Freddy's Little Sister* and was all about a boy who was forced to beg on the streets because his parents had died. He needed food to look after his little sister, who was all he had in the world, but no one gave him any money and everyone was horrible. Just when you thought it couldn't get any worse, Freddy's little sister died. Then the book ended. I cried and cried and cried, and I wouldn't talk to my grandmother all evening. Eventually, she hit me because she realized I had read her special book.

If I had a brother like Freddy, my grandmother wouldn't have done that. I told John about it, and he held me so close.

♥ *See also Baked Beans; Breasts; Endings; Zest*

kitchen equipment

*J*ohn and I met through work. This is just one of the reasons we have to keep things quiet. In one of our newsletters, we ran a competition to find the top chambermaid for our client, who supplied cleaning materials to hotel chains. Third prize was a full range of nonstick saucepans. Because it wasn't very important, Brian let me organize the photograph of the girl receiving her prize, and John came along to hand the pans over as a representative of the kitchen equipment company.

It was a bit embarrassing because Maureen wasn't as pleased with her prize as I thought she should be. She even complained about how she was going to get all the pans back home on the train with her to Leicester, which I have to admit was something we hadn't thought of. Eventually, I got her a taxi to the station, and when we found she'd left the nine-inch frying pan behind, John said I could keep it, which was nicer than he should have been given the circumstances. I think it was his kindness I fell in love with first.

When John rang me up at work the next week, he sounded nervous, as if I wouldn't remember who he was. But I did. We arranged to go out for a drink that evening, and he said that if I'd forgotten what he looked like, I wasn't to worry because he always went everywhere with a full set of saucepans and this was a fairly good distinguishing mark. I was a bit puzzled until I realized this was his sense of humor. What John didn't know was that I'd asked the photographer to print out an extra copy of the pan presentation photograph and pinned it above my desk. Brian still thinks it's because it's the first job I've done by myself. He tells me he finds my enthusiasm refreshing.

♥ *See also John; Liqueur Chocolates; Objects; Vacuuming*

lesbians

Poor John. He has to put up with so much. He told me in strict secrecy that he thinks his wife might be a lesbian.

Apparently, she and her women friends touch a lot, even in front of John. They call one another things like "doll" and "poppet" and "petal," and they are always sending secret e-mails. When John comes in, Kate hides what she's writing, so he knows it is probably about him. He has to pretend not to mind; otherwise, she'll tease him.

He said the worst thing is how these women are always laughing when they are together. John told me he hardly laughs anymore. It's all work and duty as far as he's concerned. That's why he loves being with me. He can feel appreciated.

He said Kate and her friends seem to care only about having fun. He honestly thinks that if it came down to it, she would choose her friends over him.

"It's not like you and Sally," he said. "You're like

blokes. You can pick up and drop your friendship when there's nothing better to do."

I tried to talk about this with Sally, but she said that Colin lives in hope of walking in and finding Sally and me in a delicate situation together. It is his deepest fantasy. I'm so grateful John understands friendship for what it is and is not always trying to turn it to his advantage. This is so typical of Colin, and also of Sally not to mind.

💜 *See also Codes; Rude; Voyeur; Women's Laughter*

letters

Dear Kate,
   I think you should know that . . .

Dear Mrs. Hutchinson,
   Your husband and I have been . . .

To Whom It May Concern,
   John Hutchinson is in love with . . .

Dear Kate,
   I hope you will forgive me for remaining anonymous, but I am a well-wisher who . . .

Dear Kate Hutchinson,
   I have thought long and hard before writing this letter but . . .

Dear Wife of John,
   I . . .

Dear.
   Oh, dear.

♥ *See also Codes; Endings; Utopia*

liqueur chocolates

John sometimes finds it difficult to use the *L* word. We have used up the apricot liquid I won at the sex party, but the other day, he broke open liqueur chocolates on my bare skin and made a joke of it. "I l-l-l-l-l you," he said, sticking out his tongue and licking the spilled liqueur off instead of saying *love*. It was fun at the time, but I was disappointed afterward. And sticky.

Sally says the thing to do is not to nag. They get enough of that at home. "What has he bought you?" she asked. "These men just love buying us presents, don't they?"

I couldn't show her the frying pan, the set of matching cookie tins, or even the tea towel with illustrations of all the different species of fish. Even though John and I chose it together from the local fish-and-chips shop, it doesn't match Colin's presents. Not in cash terms, anyhow. I use the tea towel to wrap up the empty chocolate boxes. John says we've got a habit.

♥ *See also Glenda G-spot; Tornadoes*

love calculators

There is a Web page on the Internet that lets you type in your name and the name of the person you love, and it works out whether you are a good match or not. John and I are 67 percent compatible. Dr. Love says that we need to work at our relationship. Sally and Colin have distinct possibilities at 78 percent, but on the other hand, Colin and I are 99 percent right for each other. A match made in heaven.

When I was at school, we didn't go on computers so much, so we used pen and paper instead for these little love calculations. We'd cross out all the letters that appeared in both names and then work our way through the remainder chanting out *love* and *hate* alternately. When I tried this with John's name, we only had two letters in common, although the ones we do share spell *it*, which has to be significant. However, when I do the chant, it comes out *hate*. I don't know John's middle name, though. Maybe if I used our full names, it would come out with a more correct answer.

♥ *See also Mistaken Identity*

lust

When my father was lying in his hospital bed, I tried hard to concentrate on things he'd like to talk about. It was difficult, though, because what I couldn't say was that I felt like I was wading through an erotic fever.

The sicker he got, the more I wanted to make love to healthy men. My need was shaming. John was the first person I told about how I really felt. The men I knew at the time were too grateful to speak much. When John told me lots of people felt the same, I was so relieved. This is what I like about John—not the fact that being with him is exciting, just the opposite. John makes me feel normal.

💜 *See also Grief; Illness; Teaching; Why?*

M

magazines

*J*ohn thinks it is strange that I have never shared a flat with anyone. I did think about moving in with Sally once, but then Mum got ill, so I just stayed at home until I bought my own flat.

Besides, having a flatmate is not something I've ever fancied. It's not just all that fridge etiquette; but if I wanted to sum up everything I hate about the flatmate relationship, it's the way they read each other's brand-new magazines without asking. There is something so special about opening a glossy magazine and being the first to tear the pages when they get stuck together or try out the perfumes. A used magazine is about as appealing as a half-finished yogurt. At least I know Sally would never leave me with either.

💜 *See also Houses; Routines; Velvet*

marathons

The first time John and I had sex over the telephone, it was just a joke. Now we do it for hours. He once rang me up from the supermarket car park when he was supposed to be picking up some barbecue meat. He'd gone into the far corner where no one could see him. I felt incredibly sexy and strong, turning him on so much. I felt liberated.

I told him we'll have to get each other those special hands-free headsets for Christmas. He said we will get so used to talking about sex that when we finally get together, we will have to have separate phone lines installed in the house so we can carry on doing it this way.

When we finally get together.

I didn't say anything at the time, but I was desperate for him to get off the line so I could phone Sally. When I did, I could tell from her tone that Colin had never said anything like that to her.

♥ *See also Boxing; Endings; Heroines; Jealousy; Ultimatum; Why?; Youth*

mars bars

Sally and I used to buy Mars bars from the school store. Then we would wrap them in wet flannels and put them on the radiator so they'd get a mottled, almost moldy look. We became experts at writing disappointed complaint letters to the company using different names, and we'd get sent large selection boxes in recompense. It was fine at first, but the trouble was that we got greedy and the company got the school store shut down because they had received so many complaints about its hygiene.

We never told anyone it was us. Especially when everyone got so annoyed about not being able to buy snacks anymore. They might have forgiven Sally, but never me.

❤ *See also Blackbirds, Robins, and Nightingales; Outcast; Vendetta*

memory

—Will you love me forever?

—I will.

—Will you ever forget me?

—Never.

—Will you remember me in one week's time?

—Of course.

—Will you remember me in one year's time?

—Definitely.

—Will you remember me in ten years' time?

—I will.

—Knock, knock.

—Who's there?

—See, you've forgotten me already.

—Jesus, woman, just let me read the paper, can't you? This is worse than being with the kids.

—

—Verity?

—

—Verity, oh, Verity, darling. Stop crying. I didn't mean it. I'll remember you forever. I promise. I'll love you forever.

❤ *See also Endings*

mirrors

A funny thing happened when I looked in the mirror this morning.

I saw I had tilted my head slightly to the left without thinking, and for a minute, it was my mother looking back at me. I was even making that half smile she made every time she looked in the mirror, as if she were greeting someone she hadn't seen for a long time.

This might be a sign of age. I have noticed that the older women at work always put their heads to one side when they look in the mirror. It's as if they're afraid of what they'll see if they face themselves straight on.

❤ *See also Daisies; Horror Movies; Mistaken Identity; Old;*
  Voyeur; Zzzz

mistaken identity

I once pretended to be my mother on the telephone. I didn't mean to do it. It was just that the person on the other end automatically assumed I was Mrs. Bell. It felt wonderful, just like when I used to take my father's car keys and walk up and down swinging them in my hand, hoping that people would think I was old enough to own a car. I started to feel that if only I really could take my mother's place, everything would be all right. I would have somewhere to go where I could be me.

Maybe this is what we always feel about mothers. Their very presence stops us being us. Maybe this is why I hate Kate so much.

From what John says, she has always put being a mother first. She has been too busy with the kids to spend any time with him for a long time. She has no idea of how much he needed her, and now they have nothing in common but the children. I can't help thinking this is the wrong thing for her to do when mothers are so easily replaced.

♥ *See also Daisies; Engagement Ring; Illness; The Queen II; Stepmothers; Underwear*

money

Not many people know that if you put a two-pound coin in the freezer and wait until it is completely frozen, you can then press the middle bit out with your thumbs.

Mind you, this makes it difficult to use, so you can do this only if you have money to spare.

John has started talking about money a lot. It makes me feel uncomfortable because we have such different ideas about it. He thinks if he ever had any spare cash, it would be his duty to spend as much of it as he could. Not just on himself, but on making other people happy. I told him that when I was young, I always used to be very helpful to old people on buses because I thought they might then leave all their money to the little girl who was so kind to them. Every time I heard the doorbell ring, I would wonder whether this was my reward coming. Now John says that he wants money so he can leave it to a complete stranger when he dies. Maybe someone whose name he pulls out of a phone book at random and who will always be perplexed by why he or she was chosen.

❤ *See also Love Calculators; Surnames; Utopia*

money — even more of it

Of course, when my parents died and left me an inheritance, I knew why they chose me. I just didn't expect it to be so much. Money wasn't something we ever talked about at home. Even the solicitor was surprised. He kept going on about the Responsibility. About how I was almost an "heiress" now. It made me think of Joan Crawford somehow. All hard and glittery but with ample shoulder pads to bear all that Responsibility.

Everyone was so kind to me after my father passed away. Sally took me home, and I slept in her family's spare bedroom for a week. Her mother made me cups of tea, and her father teased me, and every time I cried, they thought it was because I was sad about my parents. They didn't realize it was because I was so comfortable there. This is what I wanted for the rest of my life. And I couldn't bear the guilt of that.

This is why I don't want the money. It changes everything. Sally's parents would have expected me to check into a hotel, not taken me under their wing like they did. So I worked it out with my solicitor that no one need know anything about it. We've let out my parents' house through a letting agency, and what with that and the income from my stocks and shares, I don't need to worry about anything anymore. He even gives me pocket money as if he's my father. He insists I go to his office every month to go through things, although I trust him absolutely and only pretend to check the figures.

The trouble is, you can't go to bed with money. It can't hug you and stroke you and tell you that everything is going to be all right. As soon as you have it, it covers you up, so everyone expects you to take charge. To be the one to tell everyone else that everything is going to be all right. To take the Responsibility.

In fact, my solicitor is the only person who knows about the legacy. Sometimes if I try very hard, I can forget about it myself. I can even enjoy dreaming with John about how we would spend our imaginary millions. This has become one of our favorite topics of conversation. Sometimes I wonder if it is what holds us together. We have such plans that would all come true if only we had the money.

♥ *See also Danger; Jealousy; Teaching; Velvet; Yields*

mustache

I had the idea to make a giant heart out of chicken wire and fill it with white fairy lights as a surprise for John. I went to the hardware shop to get the stuff but wasn't sure what wire cutters to buy. When I asked some-

one, I suddenly found myself surrounded by four men of-
fering me different advice. They were all very interested in
what I was doing, and two of them even offered to come
round and help me if I hit problems.

On my way home, it struck me that I had stumbled
onto something important. Women spend all this time
and money on finding Mr. Right. What they don't realize
is that men are there all the time, lurking in the aisles of
DIY shops. All you have to do is buy wire cutters.

I think I am finally coming to understand the secrets
between men and women. John was feeling around my
face with his fingertips the other night. He traced the outline of my nose, pressing the end with his thumb. He told
me that his mother used to do this when he was a little
boy so he would have a round nose like hers and not his
father's beak.

He then rested all his fingertips over my upper lip. "I
love your mustache," he said. I felt myself go tense, especially when he leaned forward and dolloped out little
butterfly kisses all over my face. Was he joking?

I pushed him away. "What's wrong?" he asked. He
really couldn't understand.

"I haven't got a mustache," I said. "Men have mus-
taches, not women."

"But you've got such a wonderful one," John said. "It's
beautiful. You've no idea how it turns me on. I wish you
wouldn't pluck out the hairs like you always do."

I couldn't believe it. I have spent so many years trying
to hide the fact that I have facial hair, and here was someone telling me it was sexy. My stomach turned over with

love for John. If only men would realize that this is all women need. To be desired without boundaries, to be loved for all the things we have got wrong with us, not for what we would like to be.

❤ *See also Hair; Vacuuming; Women's Laughter*

mystery tours

My father was brought up in a cathedral city, and when he used to take Mum off for their little holidays, I would stay with my grandparents there. In the cathedral, there was an effigy of a dead body that had been carved after the body was buried and dug up. It had worms coming out from its skull. My grandmother would always take me to see it and then leave me there while she went shopping.

As another special treat, we would go to the department store where there was a cage of stuffed birds. If you put a penny in, they would come to life and sing to you. I got told off once for hitting a small boy who just stood by, watching the birds sing, while I used up all my pocket money. Maybe, my grandmother said afterward, he didn't have any money and that was his only chance of happiness. "Don't you feel guilty because you have so much?" she asked me.

I thought about this a lot, and even though I didn't have any dessert that day, I was still glad I hit him.

Once she took me on a mystery tour. We had to get on a coach in the town center first thing in the morning, and we didn't have a clue where we were going. The coach was full of old people, and my grandmother kept telling me how exciting it was. We went down so many bumpy roads, I started to feel sick, but we drove and drove and drove until we came to a pub and the coach driver got out and had a drink. My grandmother bought me a warm lemonade and some crisps, and then when I went to the loo, a wasp drowned in my lemonade. I couldn't have another because it was time to drive back home. When I called my parents that evening, my grandmother shouted to me that I should tell them what fun we had. So I did.

For years afterward, everyone kept telling me how much I enjoyed mystery tours until I nearly believed them.

♥ *See also Dreams; Jealousy; Kisses; Underwear*

names

My father told me that when he was growing up, there was a family on his road who called their sons by the days of the week and their daughters by the months of the year. They only reached June with the girls, but the boys went right through the week. My father's particular friend was called Saturday Smith.

We used to talk about names a lot in our family. That's what made me realize how much they matter. Once my father hit the dining-room table with the flat of his hand because he'd got into a blind rage about why someone would call their child James James. That's what got me thinking that maybe your name becomes more important than something you just have dangling down from your body, like a scarf or a handbag. Your name gets into your lifeblood, so a Jane is always going to be different from a Mercedes. A Daisy from a Violet. A Kate from a Verity.

In which case, it worries me even more how many Conservative politicians are named Norman.

"How many people do you know called Norman?" I asked John one night. He said he knew no one personally.

"Now think how many Conservatives you can name," I said. "They even marry Normas. Is this something that happens at birth, or do you turn Conservative from years of being bullied at school?"

John told me that he was at school with someone who wanted to be a spy. This boy would never let himself be photographed in case it could be used against him later. John couldn't remember his name, even when I told him I was at school with a girl called Jackie Gotobed.

♥ *See also Codes; Surnames; Words*

new men

Sally and I agree that we could never love a new man. It's not just the sandals either. It's the lack of juice. You want to feed them raw steak. John says that what he loves most about me is the way I desire him. He says it makes him feel real. I can't talk about this with Sally. She'd think I was just a sex object for John.

♥ *See also Marathons; Phone Calls; Rude; Sex*

noddy

John was once sitting down watching television with his wife when he remembered a joke someone had told him. He laughed so much that his wife prodded him to shut up, but John was so helpless with laughter, he rolled off the sofa and onto the carpet. He sobered up then and got back up. Neither of them referred to the incident at all. They just carried on watching the program. This has worried John for a long time, which is why I try to laugh with him at the joke; but if I'm honest, I find it sad rather than funny. This is how it goes:

Noddy was going to see his good friend Big Ears. He woke up in the morning and was very excited.

"Thank you, bed," he said, "for letting me sleep so well so I can be wide awake to see my good friend Big Ears."

And then he went to the bathroom.

"Thank you, bathroom," he said, "for letting me use you so I can be well prepared to see my good friend Big Ears."

And then he went to have some breakfast.

"Thank you, kitchen," he said, "for being there so I can prepare food to give me energy to see my good friend Big Ears. Thank you, food," he said as he ate, "for filling me up so I can see my good friend Big Ears. Thank you, floor," he said as he crossed the room, "for taking me to the door so I can see my good friend Big Ears. Thank you, door," he said as he went outside, "for letting me out of the house to see my good friend Big Ears."

He went to his car. "Thank you, car," he said as he got in, "for taking me to see my good friend Big Ears."

He drove along. "Thank you, tarmac; thank you, pavement; thank you, traffic signals; thank you, map; thank you, road directions; thank you, thank you, thank you, everyone who is helping me see my good friend Big Ears."

He parked outside his friend's house. "Thank you, road, for letting me leave my car so I can see my good friend Big Ears. Thank you, gate, for opening so I can go and see my good friend, Big Ears. Thank you, path, for taking me up to the house of my good friend Big Ears. Thank you, doorbell, for letting me ring to alert my good friend Big Ears."

He waited until he could hear footsteps coming down the stairs inside the little house.

"Thank you, stairs," he whispered, "for bringing my good friend Big Ears closer and closer to me."

At last, Big Ears opened the door.

"Fuck off, Noddy," he said.

♥ *See also Doors; Houses; Liqueur Chocolates; Youth*

normals

Last summer Sally and I were on a train when we noticed that the two men in the seats across the aisle had not looked at us once.

This was puzzling.

I thought they must have been trainspotters, but Sally listened to their conversation for a bit. It turned out that what they actually spotted was the stations. They rode on trains every day, choosing lines that took them through the most number of stations. Then they wrote the names down in a big book.

We couldn't stop laughing. Every time we thought we'd got it under control, the train would glide past some deserted platform with one of those swinging signs, and we'd hear the shuffle of papers opposite us and we'd be off again. We were crying and making little squeaks like baby pigs. Sally's nose was starting to run.

The men did look at us then. One of them even shrugged and spat out the word *normals*.

I asked Brian about this the next day. He said that a friend of his who sometimes liked to go trainspotting—well, anyway, this "friend" had heard that people who didn't like trainspotting were called "Normals." I couldn't explain to Brian why I found this insulting. I just did.

He told me then that naturists—and another "friend" of his apparently has been known to go to nudist beaches—called people who wore clothes "Textiles." He kept on about this for the rest of the day as if it were a joke both of us shared.

"How are you doing, Textile?" he'd shout across from his desk.

The trouble with Brian is that he doesn't know when he has taken things too far.

♥ *See also Bosses; Firefighting; Glenda G-spot; Words; Zero*

n o s t r i l s

S ophia found me crying in the ladies' room at work. Of all the people to see me at my worst, she would be one of the last people I'd pick. It's not just the fact that she is the company accountant. It's her nostrils. They're more on show than anyone else's. It's as if she's put two fingers up her nose and turned it inside out. Her nostrils are long and stretched, and the skin's boiled red inside. It's difficult to look at Sophia and think of anything else. I would hate to see Sophia with a cold. Just the thought of it makes me feel physically sick.

Sophia took me by the hand and led me into her office. She put me in a chair in the corner of the room and just ignored me. Eventually, I stopped sobbing and stood up.

"It won't be the last time it happens," she said, barely looking at me. "And every time it does, you will think this really is the end, that this time you'll never get back with each other, and your heart will break again and again until you don't think you can bear it anymore. But I promise you that you've a long, hard journey ahead. You won't be able to leave each other alone, and it will hurt just as much each time one of you decides that you must part."

"How did . . ."

"Oh, I don't know the details of your particular relationship," she said. "But I do know about pain indexes, believe me. And men. He won't be worth it. They never are."

Then she handed me a mirror before going back to her columns of figures.

"You'd better freshen up," she said. "You look a mess."

I stared at my reflection. My eyes were puffy and red, but who was she to call me a mess? At least I have always been lucky with the shape and size of my nostrils.

💙 *See also Friends; Kindness; Wrists*

nursing

*I*f I could change just one thing about John, it would be the way he is always complaining about being ill. Last Monday, for example, he was moaning about a pain in his arm.

"It is either a strain from all the gardening Kate made me do over the weekend or the last stages of a cancerous tumor," he whinged. I tried to take his mind off it, but I noticed he kept rubbing the spot and looking worried, as if he might die at any minute.

I told Sally about it. I shouldn't have done that because she kept mocking John, rubbing her forehead and saying that either she was bored with talking about him or she was in the last stages of a terminal tedium. But then she had a good idea.

Now, whenever John complains about being ill, I am incredibly sympathetic. I tell him he should tell Kate to massage him gently for a long time or to cook him special meals or to go buy him expensive and elusive medicines.

"Do you think so?" he asks, hopefully.

"I do," I say. "I think this is something she needs to take very seriously indeed. I would, if I were her."

💙 *See also Illness; Stationery; Teaching; Women's Laughter*

objects

*J*ohn told me that he went round his house last night looking at all the objects he and his wife had bought together. He said he was ticking things off in his mind.

If I go, I'll take this, this, and this.

That, that, and that will stay.

It was a terrible thing to do, he said, because he realized that was all a marriage comes down to in the end. Objects. Even the children, he said. Even the children would be shared between him and Kate.

I held him close and told him that if I had him, I would never need anything else. We stayed like that, in each other's arms, for a long time. We were silent because he was upset, and all I wanted to ask was whether he was going to take the painting of beach huts by the sea that we once took to be reframed together.

I have always liked that painting.

❤ *See also Houses; Money; Property; Questions*

old

*M*y heart is breaking. All I can see in front of me is a dark, black corridor with nothing making it worthwhile to come out the other side. John can't bring himself to think about leaving Kate anymore. He says it would kill her. Apparently, she's spent too much of her life relying on him, and he has to accept the responsibility. Plus, he'd feel so guilty that he'd taken the best years of her life. Maybe if they'd both been younger? Younger like me. He told me that I'd be all right, that I had my whole life ahead. I had to live well, to make him proud.

I felt numb. He was crying when he said all this, so I told him it was all right, that I understood, but the next day I was having a sandwich in a local coffee shop when I realized the woman sitting opposite me must be in her early forties, probably exactly the same age as Kate. I knew it wasn't her, but I couldn't stop staring at this woman. She was reading some papers, an important-looking document, so I felt I could stare all I wanted without her noticing me.

I was trying to see what it was like to be that old. She had all the usual imperfections, but when I looked closely, I saw some I hadn't thought of before. The skin at the sides of her face was puckered round her ears, as if it needed stretching. Then when she turned round to pick her coat off the back of the chair, I saw she had lines at the back of the neck as thick and deep as the thin gold chain she was wearing. The areas around her eyes were black, not just underneath as you get sometimes from lack of sleep, but at the edges of her nose, right up to her eyebrows too, so her sockets looked sunken.

John told me once that what Kate hated most about getting old was the fact that she felt she was becoming invisible. John said that Kate was losing all her confidence and bounce. This was another thing that made him feel guilty.

I could see that the woman sitting opposite me at the table was nervous. She apologized when other people bumped into her, she kept giving me silly little smiles, she tried to make conversation with the man who came to clear away the table even though he wasn't interested. When I saw her start to put her things away to go, I knocked over my coffee on purpose, willing the dark brown liquid to spill over her papers.

"I'm sorry," I said as she whipped everything up quickly, trying to take care of the worst of the damage with a sodden paper napkin. "I just didn't notice you there."

The woman looked as if she was trying not to cry. The manager came rushing over. He was about twenty-five, as dark and handsome as an Italian film star. I smiled at him, and he stopped in his tracks for a moment, then smiled back. Together we watched the woman flutter her hands here and there until he remembered what he was there for and started to wipe the papers with the wet cloth in his hands.

"Don't." She was almost shouting. "These are important. They're Work things." That's how she spoke. Gave *Work* a capital letter, as if that was all she had in her life. All she had left to her. After she'd gone, I watched the other people in the café give one another little smiles. I hoped she'd get into trouble when she got back to the office. I felt no guilt. Didn't she know it was women her age who were ruining my life?

The next night John came round and said he was wrong. That he couldn't let me go. That he'd see a way of making things all right. I made a point of lifting up my hair and asking him to kiss the back of my neck. I told him women loved that, because I guessed he sometimes tried out things we did with Kate. "Is it smooth?" I asked. "Are there any lines there?" He whispered into my skin that I was beautiful, flawless, a national treasure. I turned my head round so his mouth was against my cheek, just by my ear.

"I really couldn't bear to be lined and ugly," I said. "I'll be perfect for you forever."

He smiled, but something was wrong. It was the first time I'd been with John and felt guilty. He kept poking his tongue at my skin until I had to push him off.

💜 *See also Breasts; Endings; Mistaken Identity; Youth*

o m e l e t

My mother always used to say that it was impossible to make an omelet without breaking eggs. It seemed substantial at the time, like something I should listen to, but I can't help wondering what it all meant now. Of course you need to break the eggs. It's just common sense.

💜 *See also Elephant's Egg; Endings; Old; Questions; Voices; X*

omens

The world has become a more interesting place since I fell in love.

A magpie flying overhead used to be just a black-and-white bird. It is now a sign that today is going to be awful, so I have to spend the next hour searching for another to balance it out. Two birds flying together fills me with joy. It means that John really does love me. That we're going to be happy together forever.

That black cat crossing the road . . . the chimney sweep . . . the four-leaf clover. If I go into a pub and count ten blond-haired men, if the sandwich I've picked with my eyes shut turns out to be chicken, if I can get to that shop without seeing a red car. . . .

If.

♥ *See also Horoscopes; Love Calculators; Telephone Boxes; Utopia*

only children

Sally and I are both only children. John is the youngest of three. He has two children of his own. There are bound to be things he can't understand about me that Sally can.

There is a responsibility about being an only child. On the one hand, you are the most wanted person in the universe, the one who completes the family, the little plastic figure who makes living in the dollhouse worthwhile. On the other, you bear single-handedly the pressure of changing someone's life beyond recognition. When things go wrong, it can be no one else's fault but yours.

This is a lot for a child to have to cope with.

There was a psychological experiment once. They put a group of strangers in a room and forbade them to speak to one another. Then they asked them to circle round, just looking, until they found someone they wanted as their potential partner. They all chose, but remember they hadn't spoken yet. When they finally got to talk to their partner, the vast majority found that they had paired up with someone who shared the same place in the family as they did. Youngest child with youngest child, older with older, middles with middles. I like to think the experiment finally ended when the only children were peeled off the outside walls and forced to join in with the rest. Maybe they would then have made cynical comments about the easy comradeship of the other people there, but more likely, they would have got into an argument as to who had the unhappiest childhood.

♥ *See also Ants; Blood; Captains; Daisies; Questions; Relatives; Zzzz*

oranges

I knew a girl once who used to say that if you ever wanted to pick anyone up, all you needed to do was to go on a train journey with a copy of *Rebecca* and a large apple. You would have hardly nibbled through the skin, or even reached Manderley, before a man approached you.

I tried it with John one evening, but all I had in the fruit bowl was oranges. John was watching football, and he didn't even look at me, just passed me his hankie so I could mop the juices off my chin. He says it's a compliment to how relaxed he feels with me that he can spend the little time we have together watching television.

Besides, it was an important match that he was supposed to be watching down at the pub with his friend Sam.

♥ *See also Endings*

orphans

I have been an orphan for two years now. It's difficult to say that without sounding pathetic, but my friends are now my family. Well, John is now my family.

No, I am completely happy. I miss nothing. I am searching for nothing. Especially not a father figure. Sally is wrong. She is just jealous because although Colin has more money, he does not treat her as well as John looks after me. I can tell John everything. And I do. He says he wants to protect me so carefully that no harm will ever happen to me. This is why I have to do what he says, be what he wants. Everyone needs someone to look after them.

♥ *See also Stepmothers; Teaching; Voices; Zzzz*

outcast

*U*ntil we started on her, Dawn was no different from any other girl at school.

But then one day in the lunch hall, she dropped her tray. It was full of food, but while embarrassing, even that might have been all right on its own. After all, it was something we worried about doing ourselves. But then, instead of cursing or picking it up or doing anything, Dawn just stood there, blushing. Soon she was completely red.

Dollops of shepherd's pie in greasy gravy lay around her feet. Chunks of tinned pineapple, banana, peach left snail trails on the floor where they'd skittered away from the shattered bowl.

After the initial thud, the dining hall was completely silent. Everyone was watching Dawn. I felt my stomach well up and get stuck in my throat. Why didn't she do anything? My head seemed to be expanding beyond my skull. I wanted to scream.

I don't know who it was who first started to clap, but soon we were all joining in. That slow clap-clap-clap, each one separated by a heartbeat's silence. Even the teachers seemed frozen, until Dawn spun round and ran out of the hall. She must have kept on running through the school and into the street because the next time we saw her, she was standing next to her father as our form teacher told us all about how we must be kind to everyone, regardless of their background. How we mustn't ostracize Dawn just because she was not like us.

We stared at Dawn, trying to work out what was wrong with her background. I honestly don't think anyone had noticed anything special about her before. It was then that we saw the hole in her cardigan at the elbow, the dirty socks, the smudges on her face not wiped off by a mother's spit. She was looking down at the ground as if to give us a better view of the scruffy parting of the hair, not painfully sculpted each morning like our mothers did with the sharp end of the comb.

Then we started on her father. We asked ourselves what was he doing there in school when all our fathers were at work. Why was he in dirty old jeans and a V-necked jumper without a shirt, let alone a tie? We saw him looking at us all, not defiantly, but with eyes full of what we could recognize even then as defeat.

I can't remember anyone ever talking about it, but I can't have been the only one who felt my blood rise at how they could just stand there and take the humiliation. We became pack animals, the rest of us, trying to rid ourselves of the weakest links.

Dawn never had a happy day at school again after that. Sometimes she tried to talk to me because I was left on my own at playtime too, but I'd turn my back on her.

Couldn't she see being hated was something two people could never have in common?

🖤 *See also Captains; Start-rite Sandals; Vendetta*

pain index

*I*f John and I were together all the time, I know we would be able to speak normally to each other. The trouble is, when we speak on the telephone now, I have a second conversation—the things I really want to know—going on in my mind. This makes it difficult to talk, so when I do eventually say what I want to say, it comes out too quickly and harshly and I start crying.

John says he can't bear it. He just wants things back to being as they were. He says I need to find a way round this.

❤ *See also Nostrils; Utopia*

phantom e-mails

*T*he first time I e-mailed myself, it was just a joke. To see what would happen. I wrote:

Dear Verity,

You are my life. Every time I wake up, I wish you were next to me. Nothing is worth us being apart.

And then one click of a button and it was gone. I forgot all about it, but the next time I checked my e-mails, I felt a rush of joy when I saw there was one waiting for me in my in-box.

It was everything I could have wanted. Brian must have seen the smile on my face because he started teasing me. I had to admit that, yes, I had just received a wonderful note. "You are my life," I whispered to myself. For the rest of that day, everyone was nicer to me than they usually are. I think they wanted to rub a little of my joy off onto their own lives.

I kept checking all day, but there wasn't another e-mail. Late at night, after a bottle of wine, I went on the Internet again. By the time I got into the office in the morning, there were three e-mails waiting for me, each one as magical as the first. This has made me see what I'm missing in my life, and how easy it would be to make it happen.

♥ *See also God; Mistaken Identity; Zero*

phone calls

Since I've started receiving the e-mails, I've been feeling better. I've also had more courage about contacting John at work. I rang him up once when I knew he was in a meeting. I imagined his little office full of people talking about kitchen equipment.

"I can't stop wanting you," I said. "Do you want me too?"

He told me yes, he believed he did.

"Would you like to make love to me now, on the carpet, with everyone looking?" I asked. He said that that would be a consideration and that he would think about it very hard when it was more convenient.

"I'd take off all my clothes," I said, "and climb on your lap. You'd be wearing your suit, but I'd be able to feel how much you wanted me through the material. I'd rub my bare skin all over you."

He said that this was definitely a matter he needed to spend more time on. He wondered if it would be possible for us to talk about it later. When we could take it further. In more depth. Perhaps there were other angles he needed to investigate.

I put the phone down then. When we did talk about it later, he told me that he suddenly realized that he was cradling the receiver like a baby and stroking the telephone cord like it was my hair. Everyone in the room, he said, was staring at him.

He made me promise never to do it, ever again, but that night we made love for such a long time, he missed his train home and had to get a taxi.

❤ *See also Codes; Marathons; Teaching; Vacuuming*

pop stars

L ast week after we'd made love, John told me that when he was a teenager, people used to think he looked like David Bowie. He asked me which pop star I used to fancy when I was young. The phrase sounded so odd and old-fashioned coming from him like that. *Pop star. Fancy.* I wanted to giggle.

We were in bed. John had his eyes shut, and the way he was lying against the pillow made him look as if he had a double chin, so I found a little spot on the ceiling to concentrate on instead.

Did I like David Cassidy or Donny Osmond? he asked, because in his experience, girls usually went for one or the other. Although, of course, he went on, his eyes still shut, if a girl was really cool, she'd go for Bryan Ferry. Kate had liked . . .

By the time I turned to him, his eyes were wide open and he was watching me.

It's important to be able to talk about everything, I told him. But when I said who I'd liked when I was a teenager, he said he'd never heard of him.

I wonder if that spot on the ceiling is damp. The people above have probably let their bathwater flow over. Sometimes they have no consideration. I keep watching it now every time John and I go to bed. I could swear it's getting bigger.

❤ *See also Youth*

positive thinking

My mother was a great believer in the power of positive thinking. Her idea of a self-help book would be called *Buck Up and Sort Yourself Out*. I tend to agree with her, so why did I spend £8.99 at lunchtime on a book called *How to Keep Your Man*? I can't stop thinking about Kate. Has she no self-respect?

❤ *See also Happiness; Imposter Syndrome*

poverty

*J*ohn says we would be very poor if we lived together. I still haven't told him about my inheritance. Instead, I tell him that I know what it is to be poor.

After all, my father often told the tale about how when he was young, his family didn't have enough money to buy him any clothes so he could never leave the house. But then when he was eighteen, they saved up enough money to get him a cap so he could look out of the window.

Actually, I don't think that story is true. But I do believe this one. My father's family scraped up enough money to buy him one good coat for school. They were so proud the day he went off wearing it that they all stood in the road to watch him go. But at lunchtime he didn't come back. Eventually, my grandmother went up to the school to find him, and he was in the changing rooms crying because someone had stolen his brand-new coat. There was only one coat left hanging up, but it was too big and very, very scruffy. Because she was so cross, my grandmother made my father wear it, and his own new coat was never found.

John's grandmother used to make clothes for the gentry. One day she had to make jackets for the local hunt. She used what material was left over to make winter coats for her children, including John's mother. All the other children used to tease them, but the material would never wear out because it was of such good quality. It was hunting pink.

I held John close after he told me that story. When I think of my father now, a picture of John comes into my mind. He's in a very big pink coat, and he's this little shrimp, all lost and white-faced, looking out.

♥ *See also Fashion; Indecent Exposure; Objects*

promotion

hen you are happy, good things happen to you. It's all a question of attitude.

We were asked for suggestions as to how we could improve the atmosphere at work. John had just rung me up to tell me he loved me. I felt like I could rule the world.

Why not turn the downstairs storeroom into a staff café? I wrote. Bring in plates of sandwiches every lunchtime, put jugs of fresh orange juice on the tables, have coffee machines so people can help themselves to fresh coffee. We can talk to one another about work, relax, forge a communal atmosphere, even invite clients there.

Now everyone keeps coming up and telling me what a good idea it was. The chairman even stopped me on the stairs and asked how I was enjoying my job. Brian says I'm bound to get a promotion. I just need to keep up the good work.

John hasn't phoned me at all today. I have just spent an hour typing out *John call Verity. John call Verity,* over and over again. It's an attempt at mind reading, but in reverse. A whole pile of work I'm supposed to be getting through is lying abandoned at the back of the desk. People are starting to get cross with me. Brian keeps harrumphing at me from the other side of the room.

The trouble with the staff café is that I will have to spend my lunchtimes at work now. I won't be able to sneak out and meet John.

♥ *See also Bosses; Positive Thinking; Zero*

property

I know exactly what road John and I will live on.

I walk down there regularly checking out our new neighbors. I've worked out which ones John and I will be friends with. I even plan the little dinner parties we will hold.

Once the front door of a house in the street was left open, so I looked inside. All I could see was the hall, but that was painted a cheerful yellow color, which seemed a good sign.

I stood there and tried to imagine just what my life could be like, if I lived there. I could hear the low murmurs of us talking in bed at night, smell the food I would cook for John, taste his lips when I kissed him good morning, feel his suit jacket brush against my skin when he left each morning for work. In the background, I could even make out other voices, children's voices, like shadows in the wind.

After a while, a woman came out of the house, stared at me, and slammed the door shut. I felt bereft but couldn't move. A bit later, I saw her face in the bedroom window.

I knew she was wondering whether to call the police. I wanted to tell her, *Don't.*

That we would be friends soon.

It was like the sun going out. Seeing that navy blue door shut out the bright yellow of mine and John's future. There was something so final about it.

♥ *See also Omens; Stalking; Utopia; Yellow*

the queen

T he Queen thinks the world smells of fresh paint be- cause everywhere she goes is freshened up especially for her.

John thinks I wear black lace underwear every day. He says it's such a change from Kate, who makes no effort.

"It's important," I tell him, "not to take anything for granted."

♥ *See also Breasts; Underwear; Zest*

the queen II

W hen I was sixteen, I went to Ireland with my par- ents on the ferry. We had just sat down to our fish-and-chips when a loudspeaker announcement said that the Queen was on a boat nearby and that the captain would be obliged if all passengers could go up on deck to wave to her. We ran upstairs, but when we got there, it was just the *Britannia* with all the sailors in white saluting at us. My mother said she could see the Queen, but neither I nor my father believed her.

We had just got back to our meal when there was another loudspeaker announcement. The Queen was really there this time, it said. We made our way up more slowly. The Queen was on a motorboat, being taken back to the *Britannia* at high speed. She was wearing a green coat and dress with a matching hat, and she was standing up straight in the boat, but because it was going so fast and the sea was choppy, she waved to us so oddly that she looked like a mechanical puppet.

Later, my father said it was not her but a cutout doll, but my mother told him not to be so stupid. Nevertheless, it was, my father said, a lesson in not taking things at face value.

When I asked him what he meant, he said that the Queen probably thought that our waving to her from the ferry was an outbreak of spontaneous applause because we loved her so much.

I've thought about this since. Surely no one could be that stupid.

Or could they?

♥ *See also Friends; Sex; Ultimatum; Zest*

questions

What would you do?

John keeps asking me this. He's talking about his children. What should he do about them? I know what he wants. He wants me to make his mind up for him. But John is a Libra. If I tell him what I think, he will immediately start to see the other side. I will be in the wrong whatever I say.

I told him to divide a piece of paper into two and write down the pros and cons of leaving on each side. He came through hours later and said that the trouble was that the children mean everything to him. I felt he'd hit me.

"So do I mean nothing to you?" I asked.

"No," he said. "You mean everything to me too."

And then he started to cry.

♥ *See also Horoscopes; Objects; Old; Tornadoes; Utopia; Vacuuming*

quick

John has no sense of time. In this he is just like my mother. A strange thing I have noticed is that people who have no sense of time are always talking about it. They say things like "in a minute," "quickly," or "I'll get it to you soon," but the lengths of their minutes, quicklys, and soons are very different from those in the rest of the world.

I can't help thinking it is deliberate. Leaving only five

minutes to catch a train or bus gives the same adrenaline rush to some people as bungee jumping or walking along a high wall does to others. Whereas for most normal people being late is an inconvenience, for those like my mother and John it seems to give them a sense of power, in the same way as spending too much money or leaving a lover's letter out where it can be read allows people to live dangerously but within the controlled limits they have set for themselves. This way, they are the architects of their own disasters.

Once I realized this, I felt better about John. I tried to forgive my mother, too, for all the times she'd left me waiting at parties when all the other children had been picked up, but I don't think that was the same thing. I think she really did forget about me when I wasn't there.

♥ *See also Illness; Utopia*

railway stations

When you are in our position, you have to be careful in public in case anyone sees you. John and I meet in the next-door town, and afterward, I get the train home. He always walks me to the station, and we shake hands. It's hard to explain, but when I get on my train after that, I feel a holy glow emanating from me. I walk to my seat as if I'm some kind of prim secretary who dreams of one day letting her hands touch her boss's hair as she hands him the beautifully typed notes.

But then I sit down and think of John going back home to Kate, and I curse.

The other day, a couple got on just when the train doors were shutting. He was about fifty, close-cut gray hair, a business suit, the sort of boxer's face you get on men who have made it to the top the hard way. She was beautiful. In her early twenties, with honey skin and lots of long dark curls. They sat back at first, puffed out from running and giggling, but then they started to kiss. After a while, I watched his hand delve into her lap. His breath became all catchy, his eyes blurry, but then just as the whole carriage started to watch, they pulled apart. Both looked out of separate windows for a bit, but then they were drawn together again. She stood up, and he guided her by the hips to sit on his lap. All us other passengers looked at one another and smiled. It was like being in the Blitz, with their lust careering round the carriage, hitting us like rifle-shot.

Eventually, though, they went out into the corridor, and we lost sight of them. The only way you could tell they had been there was by the briefcase and newspaper left in the luggage rack above their seats. When the train came to my station, I left by their corridor because I wanted to catch sight of them. They were pinned up against the train door, wrapped in their coats, and moving so slowly and gently that it seemed they were in a dream. I thought about it all night.

The next day at the station, just as John went to

shake my hand, I pulled him to me and kissed him properly.

When I got on my train and took my seat, I hoped everyone in the carriage had been watching.

❤ *See also Marathons; Toys*

reasons . . .

. . . why Kate and John got married:

1. She was pregnant.
2. They'd known each other for years and years.
3. Their parents were good friends.
4. They liked the same food, the same books, films, music. It was easy.
5. It seemed like a good idea at the time.
6. The usual.

(Imagine that—Princess Kate pregnant before they got married!! I tried not to look shocked for John's sake. Just a bit prim, so he'd know that this was something I'd never do. But then I got to thinking. What is the usual? What *is* the usual? Why do people get married? Especially two people who have never really loved each other.)

❤ *See also True Romance*

relatives

John has twenty-seven first cousins. It is difficult to imagine what it must be like to come from such a large family. I have two cousins. That is enough. Even when my mother and father were alive, we didn't see much of them. My mother made sure of that. It's not surprising that we don't keep in contact now. I often think that we might meet up one day and not know one another. Blood is a funny thing.

In my magazine the other day, there was an article about odd relationships. There was one woman who first met her future husband when he was eight years old and a guest at her son's birthday party. They didn't marry then, of course, but it's freaky to think she must have had her eye on him all that time. Another family consisted of two sets of identical twins who got married. Their children, therefore, were genetically brother and sister even though they were really cousins.

It makes you think, doesn't it? I know, for instance, that your cells renew themselves after seven years, so would it be possible for your seventeen-year-old clone to marry your twenty-four-year-old self? They would be completely different people. I try to talk about all this with John, but he only starts making silly jokes. He says he has had enough of reproducing himself forever, particularly at four o'clock in the morning when his children sometimes wake him up.

I've never really wanted to have children. I can't imagine what it must have felt like for my mother to have me squirming away inside her stomach. Like an alien.

💙 *See also Only Children; Stepmothers; Thomas the Tank Engine; Underwear*

r e v e n g e

he chairman has been bringing his dog into the office every day now. It sits underneath his desk, and Monica has even seen it sitting in the passenger seat of the chairman's car when he goes home at night.

It turns out that the chairman's wife tried to poison it using some doctored bacon. She was jealous because the chairman spent all of his time with the dog, feeding it tidbits, calling it beautiful, and whispering secrets to it while fondling its ears.

We know this because the chairman's wife left a message at the reception desk one day saying she would have felt better if the chairman had been as besotted with their bloody au pair. Brian says he bets the bloody au pair is probably a little bit more careful about what she eats in that house these days.

💙 *See also Dogs; Tornadoes; Vacuuming; Wobbling*

rochester

Sally and I often talk about books.

We are searching for role models, but so far we have not found a second wife in literature who manages to keep her husband whole and healthy. We make lists of what physical deformities we would be prepared to accept—a burned Max de Winter versus a blind Mr. Rochester. Sally says she'll take ingrown toenails as long as he isn't wallet-less, but I'm secretly coming to terms with the idea of a limbless, sightless, and depressed John.

♥ *See also Endings; True Romance; Utopia*

routines

Only six months passed between my mother dying and my father getting ill. It wasn't a coincidence. He always had a strong will. The way he got through my mother's death was by developing a rigid pattern that held him up, even when he collapsed.

He ate the same things each day, wore particular clothes on particular days, and he devised this amazing chart that contained lots and lots of boxes he had to tick off every half hour. In fact, he became so busy with the chart that it was difficult for him to find the time to speak to me toward the end.

John came to see me the other day when I wasn't expecting him. I was pleased, of course, but I kept watching the television over his shoulder because my favorite program is on on Wednesdays, and it had got to an exciting part.

"I thought you'd be happy to see me," he said eventually, "but you don't want me here."

He was right. The funny thing was that it was only when he was getting ready to go that I realized what was happening. I asked him when he was coming next. I begged him to stay. Once he was going, I'd have done anything to get him to stay.

💗 *See also Money; Utopia; Zeitgeist*

rude

Farting is rude. Passing wind is something that just happens.

Stealing another woman's husband is unforgivable. Falling in love is something that just happens.

Until you're old enough to start doing it, just even talking about sex is so rude, it makes you giggle.

Sometimes I think John has never had sex before. He gets so excited just because I tell him we can be completely free and honest with each other. He says he thanks God for the modern woman. One night he asked me to tell him my deepest fantasy.

"I'll have to think about that," I said. I wanted to tell him one that would make me seem daring and sexy but not too dirty.

But then he told me his.

He said he wanted to walk down a street late at night.

A few houses would still have their lights on, but there was one that wouldn't have the curtains drawn. He'd be able to see right in. As he walked by, he would hear the cry of *Take me!* coming from the open window. There would be an attractive couple standing there, he said, making love. The woman would see John, watch him over the man's shifting shoulder, but then the man would notice too. He'd pull out of the woman, turn, and move aside. Then the woman would move over to the window and gesture for John to come inside the house. She'd not even pull her skirt down. She'd stand there, staring at John as he opened the front gate, as the man watched too. Then John would step over the threshold, unzipping himself as he did so.

He stopped talking then. He was breathing oddly, so I patted his shoulder and said it was okay, that I didn't mind. He looked a bit surprised, but when we made love later, I didn't move. Just lay there on my back like a virgin. When I woke up in the middle of the night, I was curled up in a fetal position and I had a sick feeling in my stomach that I didn't recognize for a while. Then I remembered. It was jealousy.

Falling in love can happen to anyone. It is very different from lusting after an unknown woman.

♥ *See also Glenda G-spot; Jealousy; Lesbians; Vexed*

S

sculpture

Sally has taken up lots of different hobbies so she won't get too preoccupied with Colin. She is studying the Spanish language and desktop publishing, and she's taking two exercise classes at the local sports club. What she likes best, though, is the sculpture course she takes at night school.

She's making lots of little nude figures out of clay. She makes them for Colin, but of course he can't take them home, so they litter their flat. She says she is making their very own orgy.

Sally told me that one of the models who came into the studio had worn a wig and that this had made all the students feel more comfortable, as if they weren't looking at a real nude body after all. Apparently, they mold their pieces of clay on stands that are set up in a circle around the model, and after ten minutes, they move on to the next place, like a clock. You are allowed to sculpt only exactly what you see, and Sally started at the back. She said it was a big shock when she came round to the front and realized that her sculpture had a big hole there. Although it had a perfectly formed back.

Sally thought that was a metaphor for her life. She said that it was the same for me, too, and that we should both think hard about what we were doing. All I could think about was what color the model's wig was and how I'd never really asked John whether he preferred blondes or brunettes.

♥ *See also Hair; Sex; Worst-Case Scenario; Zzzz*

s e x

After she'd spent the hours looking at the nude model, Sally cut off some of her pubic hair and sent it to Colin through the post so he would think of her at work. She pretends she's so independent, but I can tell she's worried about him. He's not been around to the flat for a week.

She told me that she's been meeting up with the girls again and that they've been talking about me.

"Let them," I said.

"They're worried about you," she said. "Trust me. You can't ignore your friends. Learn from my experience if nothing else."

I can't tell her the truth. That my experience could not be more completely different from hers if we tried.

"John's the real thing," I pointed out, and she touched my arm sympathetically.

"No man can be enough on his own. You have to make your own life," she said.

I didn't ask her how sending Colin perverted things like pubic hair is being independent. But when I got home, I started thinking. Would it work with John? I thought I'd give it a go, but as soon as I cut some off, tied the hairs in red ribbon, and put them in an envelope, I felt so dirty that I wanted to be physically sick.

Sally will never understand how different we are.

♥ *See also Friends; The Queen II; True Romance*

sounds

There are now some nights when John can stay over with me. He tells Kate that he works at the main factory in Birmingham those days. When we lie in bed before dawn, we sometimes hear a bird outside. The bird never sings when John's not there. Then all I hear are cars and the running footsteps of commuters and, in the distance, the sound of the station announcers and the trains going to London.

I found a list of the "Sounds of Earth" from the two *Voyager* spacecraft, which were sent into space in 1977, the year I was born. I e-mailed them to John:

Whales	Footsteps and heartbeats	Horse and cart
Planets (music)	Laughter	Greetings in 54 languages
Volcanoes	Fire	Train whistle
Mud plots	Tools	Tractor
Rain	Dogs (domestic)	Truck
Surf	Herding sheep	Auto gears
Crickets, frogs	Blacksmith shop	Jet
Birds	Sawing	Liftoff *Saturn 5* rocket

Hyena	Australian earthquake	A mother's kiss
Elephant	Riveter	Baby crying
Chimpanzee	Morse code	Life signs
Wild dog	Ships	Pulse

If I were to make a record of John and me, I would include that bird singing in the morning. I'd put in the sound of him pouring boiling water into coffee mugs while I just lie in bed waiting for him to come back, the little hum John makes in his sleep, the way he laughs out loud sometimes, shocking even himself, and the gasp he makes every time I touch him down there.

♥ *See also Ears; Property; Utopia*

stalking

Sally told me the other day that she hadn't seen Colin for a while. She said she didn't really mind because she's so busy, but it got me thinking. I hadn't walked up his road for a while, so I did last night.

The lights in his house were off, and when I looked into his garden, there were no toys or swings or anything. I think Colin must be a very cold person. Perhaps they are on holiday and he hadn't told her.

The funny thing is that it isn't that far from Colin's house to John's, but I couldn't bring myself to go down his road this time. I normally go later at night, when no one's on the streets and there's no chance he will see me.

Once, it was terrible. I was standing there trying to work out which room was which when I heard Kate come home. She was with a friend, and they were laughing, holding on to each other. I had to run onto their front lawn and hide in their hedge to avoid being seen. Luckily, it was pitch black. Kate kept saying what a good night she'd had and how good it had been to talk, and then they'd start laughing all over again. It took her a long time to get in the house. And then when she did, she started shouting that she was home. She must have woken up everyone.

I couldn't sleep that night for thinking of John and his children, waiting for Kate to come back. Their house had a very lonely atmosphere, but Kate seemed so happy. She was singing when she was looking for her keys, when she was yelling out that she was home.

♥ *See also Colin; Lesbians; Yard; Youth*

star quality

Brian has developed a habit of holding up his hands at cross angles to each other and looking at me through them as if he was making a frame.

It's annoying, but of course I eventually had to ask him what he was doing. He said he thought I might be of film-star material. Although I'd need a lot of work on my accent to make it appealing to the ear. Flat vowels apparently don't do it for men.

I wasn't taken in. I knew from looking at his computer

that he has been writing a film script. It is about a man from Yorkshire who is not appreciated by his family but who makes friends with a little Vietnamese orphan who lives with a rich and beautiful widow in the village. This orphan is initially the only one to see the man's true qualities, but when the little girl introduces him to the widow, they fall in love with each other. The film ends with the three of them living out the rest of their days in luxury in a big house with a large wall around it to keep out everyone who has been scared of their "otherness."

Brian leaves copies of the screenplay lying around because he wants me to ask him about it. He writes notes in the margins in large red type, saying things like *More sex?* and *God, how true!!!*

♥ *See also Mistaken Identity; Unfit*

start-rite sandals

John can't understand why I need so many shoes. I have just bought a pair of loafers made of turquoise leather that looks like snakeskin. I wish I could show them to Sally. They'd make her laugh. Or they would if she could manage to stop talking about John and how I'm best rid of him for two minutes.

I still feel cheated when I buy shoes now because it's almost too easy. When I was a child, it was such a procedure to buy shoes for kids that the store would give us a lollipop afterward. Just for surviving it. There was a special machine, and we had to stick our feet into black boxes to have X rays taken of how the bones were growing. It worries me how it really seemed to matter when you were a child whether you were a C or an E fitting, and now all shoes come in the same width. You just take them down from the shelf and squeeze into them somehow.

Because my feet were so wide, my mother used to make me have Start-rite sandals long after everyone else had given them up. I had big feet, and my shoes would flap when I walked, like a clown's. At school, the other girls would tease me and ask why I didn't just wear the shoe boxes. Or they would make rowing motions and say I was wearing boats.

I didn't have any friends at school, so I'd spend break times posting little pebbles through the holes in the leather of my Start-rites. The nuns kept coming over to make me join in other people's games, so I learned to run round and round the playground very fast so it would look as if I were involved in a complicated game and wasn't just playing on my own.

❤ *See also Fashion; Outcast; Velvet; Vendetta*

stationery

The only shop I would be perfectly happy to be locked in overnight is a stationery shop. After John, stationery is possibly my most favorite thing in the world. I can spend hours looking at all the different notebooks I can find, the colors of the pens, the way they feel in my hand, putting my fingers out to touch the softness of the paper, the fibers in the homemade papers, the shapes of paper clips, the solidness of staplers, Sellotape dispensers, hole punchers.

I make mental plans about how much better organized I would be if only I had a shelf full of home organizers, box files, and see-through plastic envelopes. How I would pin up "Things to Do" lists on the notice boards, write telephone messages and personal reminders on those little sticky pads. Keep a Biro on a piece of string by the telephone so that I've always got one near and am not struggling to find one with one hand or pretending I'm writing a complicated message down when I'm not.

I think it's a female thing. John says he's never even thought about what pen he uses, just if it works. I set him a challenge one day. Just before he left me, I asked him to buy me one of those colored pens that smell of different scents—raspberry, mint, chocolate, popcorn, bubble gum. Whatever flavor he brought back, I thought to myself, would tell me what he really felt about me.

I guessed he'd forget, but he rang me up the next day. He said that when he was going into the shop in the precinct to buy me my pen, a black cat walked in with him as if they were going shopping together. He pointed this out to the shop assistant, who looked up briefly and said, "Oh, not again."

When I asked John about the pen, he said that he'd been so shaken by the cat and the man's sanguine reaction to it that he'd started looking at the cookery books on the bargain-book table instead. The first one he'd picked up had a whole section about this special fruit pie his mother used to cook him. He then started telling me about his mother and what she had meant to him. He said he'd never really talked about her to anyone before.

I have noticed that John talks about himself a lot. We laugh about it sometimes, and I say, "And back to you," but it's something I can see might get annoying.

In fact, I dreamed about his mother one night soon after the pen debacle. She was teaching me how to make banana pie with goldfish baked through it, and when we took it out of the oven together, she handed me her white apron. Interestingly, the goldfish were still jumping up and down in the pie. I told John this, but he said only that he couldn't imagine his mother sharing a kitchen with anyone, let alone the woman who broke up his son's family. I think this is just sour grapes. John has never dreamed about his mother. I think sometimes he is just not as sensitive as me. The good thing about being in love is that I can recognize John's faults in an adult fashion. I do not always want to change him.

❤ *See also Nursing; Teaching; Vexed; Women's Laughter*

stepmothers

There was an interesting program on the radio the other night about stepmothers. How much they can bring to a child's life, how the relationship can actually be positive because both sides get better at communicating their emotions.

This is exactly what I feel. I look out of the bus sometimes and see all these mothers and daughters shopping, and I think what fun they are having. I have started to keep a list of the best shops for teenagers in London. I think the important thing is not to be a mother substitute, but to be a best friend. If you think this way, there is so much you can offer a child, particularly if they look up to you and model themselves on your behavior. The ideal stepmother is someone a child can aspire to.

💜 *See also Best Friends; Endings; Relatives; Ultimatum; Underwear*

surnames

I told John on the telephone last night how much it mattered what surname you have. I said I'd never liked my surname. Being able to change it was one of the main reasons I wanted to get married. He laughed and said he could think of better ones.

He never takes me seriously these days.

Once he rang me from a public telephone box to tell me he'd just read about a party Oscar Wilde had hosted. He'd invited lots of strangers who couldn't think why they were there, until in the middle of dinner, Oscar Wilde left the room and didn't come back. After a while, the strangers started talking and realized that what they had in common was that they all had surnames with *bottom* in them: Longbottom, Sidebottom, Greybottom. John seemed to think this was very funny, but I couldn't see the point.

It reminded me of when children at school used to boast about ringing up people in the telephone book who had silly names. I have a feeling John would do something like that. He was probably rifling through the book in the phone box looking for people with funny surnames at the same time as he was speaking to me.

I, on the other hand, was busy practicing my new signature. *Verity Hutchinson.* I have this feeling that if I write it enough times, it might just come true. I've started to underline my name now too. It makes it look much more solid.

♥ *See also Telephone Boxes; Ultimatum*

teaching

I have learned so many things since I've been with John. We stayed in a hotel together for the first time the other night, and he pointed out that I don't get out of the bath in the right way.

The funny thing is that I've never thought about it before. I've always just got out without thinking, all dripping wet, and wound myself up in towels. Sometimes I don't even bother to dry myself, just walk around like that until the water evaporates. I like the feeling of air on my skin. But this means that the bathroom is unpleasant for other people. Now I towel-dry myself standing up in the bath as the water drains out. It's a bit uncomfortable and cramped, but that way, I'm dry when I finally step out and John doesn't have to step in any unpleasant damp patches.

The other thing I have learned to do is to hold my knife and fork properly. John had to point this out several times before I got the hang of it. I haven't yet managed to blink without making the little clicking noise that drives John mad, but the other night I did sleep all through the night without dribbling because I told myself again and again so many times to keep my mouth shut that I think I was still saying this when I fell asleep.

I had no idea I had so many faults. It makes me embarrassed at how I behaved in public before I met John. He is so well mannered. I tried to thank him, but he just told me I was silly and that I worried too much about myself. He's right. John makes me feel large and clumsy, as if I'm always about to fall over my own feet. I have also noticed that when I am with John, I tend to sweat a bit more, my nose runs, and my feet sometimes have an unpleasant odor.

♥ *See also Captains; Imposter Syndrome; Zest*

telephone boxes
(three true stories)

The telephone box that John sometimes calls me from is being pulled down because, apparently, more and more people are using mobile phones. I can't help feeling as if bits of our relationship are being cut off one by one. I'm scared that soon we will disappear completely, so I suggested John should buy it and keep it as a historic monument, like Tom Jones did for the one he used to ring his wife from in Wales, but he just laughed. Still, it has made me think more seriously about telephone boxes. I keep finding out stories about them to tell John.

1. An engineer was out on his rounds in a very rural part of seaside Britain when he decided to stop for his sandwich lunch. He sat down by a telephone box perched on a cliff edge overlooking the sea. After about five minutes, the telephone started to ring, so he went into the box to answer it. It was the secretary from work, who started telling him about his next job.

"How did you know I was here?" he asked.

It turned out she had dialed him on his mobile but got the wrong number. The fact that she'd reached the telephone box he'd stopped to have his lunch next to was a complete coincidence.

2. During the great storm of 1987, a man was driving to work early in the morning when he realized the hurricane was brewing. He decided to ring his wife from a telephone box to tell her to lock all the windows and doors, but as he was talking to her, the telephone box was lifted by the wind and transported into a nearby field, where he found himself in the middle of a herd of cows.

The man's wife wasn't interested in this at all because she was still so cross about the fact that he'd woken her up and then hung up on her without saying good-bye.

3. My first French kiss was in a telephone box during a school dance. My favorite teacher, Mr. Shepherd, pretended I had a call and then followed me into the box. I

had to hold on to the sides in order to stop my knees shaking. In retrospect, it wasn't the most private place to snog your teacher because of all the glass sides. When we went back into the dance, everybody started singing "The Lord Is My Shepherd."

💙 *See also Influences; Worst-Case Scenario*

thomas the tank engine

John and I were in bed the other night, and he rolled me over on top of him and lifted me up and down.

"Chuff, chuff," he said. "This is hard work for the fat controller."

I wish he wouldn't bring his children into everything.

💙 *See also Toys*

thrush

Recently when going to the loo, I have noticed a smell like freshly baked bread. I thought it was because I was getting ready to settle down. That I was finally becoming domesticated. It made me feel like nesting.

But then John told me that he wondered whether I was infecting him. He said he hadn't known how to tell me before but that he'd developed a rash that came up after we made love. I went to the doctor, and even though it was quickly cleared up, it was still possibly the most embarassing thing I've ever had to do. And then to cap it all,

John was cross with me. He said he didn't know how he was going to bring the subject up with Kate.

I felt so guilty, I said I was sorry. But, of course, he doesn't need to tell her anything. They haven't had any relations like that for a long time.

♥ *See also Friends; Horror Movies; Old; Reasons . . . ; Rude*

tornadoes

*J*ohn was supposed to be spending Sunday with me, but Kate was ill, so he had to take his children to the National History Museum. I was so cross about this that he bought me a pet tornado from the shop there as a joke.

It's just a little plastic tube filled with water and glitter, but if you turn it quickly backward and forward, you can watch your own little twister develop. John and I can't stop playing with it. He says other people can keep their dogs, we have a tornado. He even got a book about them for me so we could find out more.

He's taken to calling me "F-5" as a nickname. This level of tornado reaches wind speeds of more than 300 miles per hour. The devastation is total. It causes homes to disintegrate, foundations to be left bare, possessions to be scattered. It has been known to wreak considerable damage even to steel-reinforced structures.

When John's not there, I hide the tornado in a drawer. It upsets me.

♥ *See also Dogs; Names; Revenge; Vacuuming*

toys

*A*pparently, vibrators have been around much longer than you would imagine. They were invented by doctors who were bored with men bringing their hysterical wives to them for treatment. To begin with, the doctors used to relieve the women by bringing them to climax manually, but then someone had the clever idea of inventing a machine to do the same job.

Much less messy and healthier all round. How those men must have congratulated themselves. They didn't realize what they had unleashed.

Monica asked me whether I remembered Jean from the sex party, and I couldn't think who she meant until she called her Cathy Come.

Evidently, Cathy had bought some of those little balls you put up yourself at the party and decided to wear them the next time she went to the supermarket. It was fine at first, rather nice and tingly, but then the sensation got worse, and by the time she got to frozen foods, Cathy couldn't stop coming. Eventually, she had to abandon her shopping cart at the checkout and try to walk home. She'd got only about a hundred yards when she found herself clinging to a lamppost, unable to move without groaning.

The funny thing was that no one who walked past her gave her a second look. She had become invisible.

♥ *See also Codes; Glenda G-spot; Glitter; Weight*

true romance

I have just remembered one of my mother's stories. At the time, I thought it was a disgusting tale and couldn't think why she'd told it. Who wanted to hear about old people in love?

My mother said she'd heard about a woman who had been married for forty years. Her husband loved her almost obsessively, and they had one of those particularly close relationships you're supposed to get with couples who don't have children.

But this woman had a secret. When she was younger and first married, she had fallen in love with an architect. He begged her to leave her husband and move in with him, but she refused. This woman and the architect tried many times to leave each other, but they were always drawn back—sometimes by an argument; sometimes by a smell, a memory, that made it impossible not to get in contact; sometimes by a bit of good or bad luck that they could share only with each other. Eventually, they came to the conclusion that their connection was stronger than them, that to sever this would be at the cost of cutting out a bit of themselves that would make it impossible to live.

However, the architect realized that if he forced the woman to leave her husband, she would come to him as a different person. All the soft edges he loved about her would have to be sawed off in order for her to survive the rift. She would have to want to come to him, leaving none of her heart with her husband. In the meantime, the lovers agreed that they would meet once a year and share a weekend of romance.

After five years, the couple were still as much in love with each other as they ever had been. They shyly admitted that these weekends had become the center of their lives, but the last night was always spent with the woman in tears. How could she leave her husband? He needed her.

The architect decided to spend the next year praying for a solution. After a few months, he felt a stirring within. One night he woke up and, in a half sleep, made his way to his drawing board. The lines he made on the plain paper were not coming from his brain, but direct from his heart.

When the couple met up, he was ready. It was with a tender proudness, a certainty, that he unrolled the drawings he had tucked under his arm. He took her hand and traced the rooms, the lightness of the proportions, the sheer originality of the house spread in front of them, with her fingers. It was his hopes for the future he was parading in front of her. How could he fail?

When the woman returned to her husband two days later, the architect sat alone and studied the abandoned drawings. The lines blurred with his tears, and he suddenly saw how he had gone wrong, how hopeless this shape had been—the clumsiness of the end wings meant it would never take flight. This was not the house she could ever want to live in with him. How right she had been. How right she always was. He found a pencil and started work again immediately.

Each year, the architect would design another house for his love to live in with him. She never did, but he didn't stop planning either. Sometimes a couple would come to his studio in order to have a house designed for them. The wife would get bored with discussions about budgets and work schedules and start to flick through the architect's plans. Always, he noticed, it would be the drawings for his love that would capture the wife's attention. There was something about them that called to the woman's heart. Once, one wife had even pulled out a plan. Had called her husband over. Had demanded that the architect design something just like this for them too. Something as romantic.

He refused, even when the couple threatened to leave and find another, more malleable architect. He realized something that night, however, as he pored over the drawings, wondering what it was that had attracted the strange woman so much, but not the one for whom he had intended this house. He realized that all the years of giving his heart on paper had had an effect. Somewhere along the line, he'd given up hope without realizing it. The drawings were without teeth now. They were pretty enough to attract those who had everything, but not daring or brave enough to be worth real risk and sacrifice.

He kept going, though. The only difference was that his subsequent drawings became more fanciful. Less believable. The woman seemed to appreciate them more. She exclaimed over tree houses, perched high in the sky. Laughed over underground tunnels, as comfortable and as traditional as a badger's set.

He took her praise, her love, for what it was and tried to make it enough. Only after she'd gone would he go back into his studio and weep over the houses he'd dragged out from somewhere deep within his body. The maps of his heart. All leading back to nowhere.

My mother had laughed after she'd told this story, but my father looked sad. He'd taken her hand and circled the center of her palm with his fingers. I remember feeling strangely angry. Why did I feel cold when I was with them, as if I were sitting in their shadow? It was partly to warm myself up that I told them how I wanted to find someone to love me like that architect. I wanted to be adored that much. My father looked at me as if he weren't seeing me at first. Then he got angry. He said that I couldn't understand anything. That the real love in the story was between the husband and wife.

♥ *See also Endings; Illness; Utopia*

ultimatum

Sally has got so tough from all this independence business that she thought it would be a good idea to tell Colin that unless he left his wife for her, she would leave him.

I could have told her this was a bad idea, but the situation is even worse than I suspected. Colin's divorce actually came through six months ago. His ex-wife has been happily living in Wolverhampton with a dental technician all this time.

I can't blame Sally for refusing to have anything else to do with Colin, even though he says he was going to tell her. He just hadn't found the right moment. The trouble is that now Colin agrees with Sally that she has to leave the flat straightaway. It seems he was more clever than her because he'd taken out only a short-term lease, whereas Sally's lodgers have got six more months in her own flat before she can get rid of them.

Still, Colin says Sally mustn't give him any second chances. He doesn't deserve them. Sally has devoted herself to him for too long.

A situation like this is particularly hard because it isn't just a romantic liaison for Sally; it's like giving in your notice at work too.

♥ *See also Ambition; Colin; Endings; Worst-Case Scenario; Yields*

u n d e r w e a r

*M*y mother took Sally and me together to buy our first bras. Afterward, she took us to the coffee shop as a treat and let us choose whichever cake we wanted. She watched us eat them, the cream oozing between our fingers, while she smoked. In my memories, my mother always seems to be circled with cigarette smoke, as if she were already fading away.

Sally couldn't wait to get to school to show her bra off, but mine felt itchy and uncomfortable. It was like that first week back to school in the autumn, when you crammed your feet into shoes after a summer of wearing open sandals. The leather was so creaky, pinch-tight, and solid all around your sole, constantly reminding you of timetables and rules.

It's become a habit of Sally's and mine now to buy our underwear together. Whereas once we used to feel more successful the more material we needed for our bras, now we spend a month's salary on garments designed to look as if we're wearing nothing.

The last time we went, Sally and I got the same set—purple silk with a silver ribbon woven through the edges. Sally said we looked like strippers. We were just walking over to the café to have our cream cakes when Sally suddenly turned to me and said, "I loved your mother." I was so surprised, I nearly walked straight into the road, but then we couldn't stop laughing, because we were both wearing the sort of lingerie that makes you long to be run over by a bus so you can make the ambulance man's day. Just like our mothers always told us.

♥ *See also Breasts; Mustache; The Queen; Velvet; Zzzz*

unfit

Several clients have complained about Brian's unreliability, so he was called in to see the managing director yesterday to be given an official warning. I have never seen anyone as angry as he was when he came out of that office. We all pretended to be busy with our work, trying

not to catch his eye, but Brian was like one of those mag-
nets attracting iron filings. All the hairs on his arms and
even his beard seemed to be standing up, spiking out from
him, forming a dark shadow.

He just sat at his desk staring at the same piece of paper. At lunchtime, I asked whether he wanted me to get
him a sandwich, but he shook his head.

"Are you sure? You have to eat, you know."

He looked up. "Do I?" he said. The funny thing is that
Brian has quite a nice face when he hasn't been drinking.

"There's always your film," I said. I was trying to
make things better.

"Christ, Verity, grow up, can't you?" he said. "This isn't
a game, you know." Then he stormed out and didn't come
back for the rest of the afternoon.

We worked in silence until it was time to go home. It
was as if all the air had been sucked out of the office.

❤ *See also Indecent Exposure; Star Quality; Wobbling*

utopia

I've noticed that the way John talks about the time
when he'll leave Kate and we'll live together has
changed.

It is now much more if-only-ish. And wonderful too. It
seems that when John and I get together, we're going to be
surrounded by light and sun and birds singing and fairies
fluttering and mermaids merring.

I don't know why, but I felt more comfortable when he

was glooming around, saying how unhappy we were going to be. At least that was realistic.

I suppose I should be looking for some way to get John's feet back on the ground, but I'm worried about Brian. He hasn't been in the office for two days. I've been covering for him with clients and have even managed to do some of the writing myself. Not even the managing director has noticed, and although I'm not sure how long I can do this, I feel a responsibility toward Brian.

♥ *See also Marathons; True Romance; Unfit; Yellow*

V

vacuuming

*J*ohn is much tidier than me. Sometimes he will come back to my flat after work, and before he even takes off his jacket, he starts cleaning up. I try not to say anything, but it drives me mad. He says it relaxes him, but I can't help thinking it's an insult. And boring.

The other day he took out the vacuum cleaner and started doing the sitting-room floor. He kept having to bend down to pick things up, and after a while, I noticed that he was still crouched on the floor even though the machine was still on.

I asked if he was all right. He lifted his head then, and his face looked as if he were bruised under the eyes.

He told me that at home when he did this, his dog

would always attack the Hoover. That he and it had fights that they both looked forward to. He said it seemed soulless, Hoovering just backward and forward on his own.

I didn't know what to say. I had expected John to be upset about the children. But animals? John knows I am allergic to them. At his family home, he has a dog, two guinea pigs, a rabbit, a three-legged cat, and two goldfish. I've noticed he has this maternal streak. He even pats our tornado in passing. I wonder how Kate puts up with it. It must be like living in a zoo.

💙 *See also Dogs; Kitchen Equipment; Sex; Stationery; Tornadoes; Utopia*

velvet

*I*n my pocket, I keep a corner cut out from the velvet curtains that hang in the spare room of Sally's parents' house. Because I took it from the hem so no one would notice, it's a rich red and not the faded, tea-stain color of the rest of the curtains.

I run my thumbnail along the fabric when I get upset. It can go surprisingly deep, and when I rub against the grain, I get a feeling not unlike when you put your tongue on the metal bit of a pencil sharpener. It's almost an electric shock but softer. I like it because it reminds me that there are other worlds out there. It's a world Sally must have running through her veins.

💙 *See also Fashion; Houses; Magazines; Money; Utopia; Zzzz*

vendetta

It is strange to think that someone could actually hate me as much as Kate would do if she found out who I was. Hate is such an active emotion. I talked to Sally about it, and she said, rather too casually, that people hated me at school. I was shocked. I knew they'd rather not play with me, but to hate me? That was something different. I couldn't think what I'd done to deserve that.

"It was your big eyes," she said, "and your hair. You were always staring at people as if you wanted to get inside them somehow. We used to think you were a witch."

I remembered the time Sally had caught me making up that rain dance. It was just something I'd seen on television, but now I was surprised at how much I liked this image of myself.

"My mother was a witch," I lied, thinking Sally would laugh at me.

"They say it's inherited. Your mother was magic," she said, and carried on reading the television guide. Sally is always round my house these days. While we were watching a film later on, I willed and willed her to go. As soon as the film finished, she picked up her bag and left.

"It's all right," she said. "I'm going." Although I hadn't said anything.

Now that he's back at work, I couldn't wait to try something similar out on Brian, but he kept catching my eye when I was staring at him and winking back at me.

💜 *See also Bosses; Mistaken Identity; Names; Voices; X-ray Vision*

vexed

J ohn's nickname for me is "Squiggle." When I write to him now, I sign it *Sxxx*. He says it makes him think of sex.

Recently, there have been times when I wonder if this is all he thinks about. I can't help being shocked by how much it is starting to bore me. I asked him the other day, for instance, if he missed me.

"Yes," he said. "I was feeling really randy this morning. I could have done with you then."

I wrote a note to Brian and signed it *Vxxx* by mistake. He looked up immediately, of course, and smiled. I had to smile back, and although I wanted to tell him he was wrong—that I wasn't really sending him kisses—he looked so happy, I couldn't.

💜 *See also Breasts; Ice Cream; Memory; Outcast; Phone Calls; Rude; Teaching*

victim

I'm very busy now, particularly as Brian has been giving me work as a thank-you for helping him out. I've been working on a new customer magazine for a company that makes industrial-sized pipes for construction companies. I came up with the title *In the Pipeline*, which Brian likes a lot. He says if the project goes well, he is going to recommend I get promoted officially to be his assistant editor on this publication, with more to come.

John wasn't as pleased as I would have liked. He thinks that Brian probably has hidden motives, but I don't think this is a very supportive attitude. John did apologize. He said that he is so frantic at work too, it just seems a shame that I can't be free in the little time he has to see me.

I tried to see his point. He has had to put up with being second best with Kate and the children for such a long time now. He can't bear for it to happen all over again.

❤ *See also Ambition; The Queen; Stationery; Utopia*

visible

The hairdresser kept asking if I was sure. Eventually, I just shut my eyes so we couldn't keep looking at each other in the mirror. I could hear how people kept coming over to watch her, picking up curls from the floor and telling me how different I would feel when it was done.

"A new person," they said.

Hair as thick as mine makes a remarkable noise when

it's being cut, like a knife sawing through bones. It got louder and louder the more she cut, until I thought I was going to have to tell her to stop. I suppose it was because I had no protection over my ears now.

At the end, I told her it looked lovely, that I was delighted, but she wouldn't stop showing me the back of my neck in the mirror. She obviously didn't believe me, but she was wrong. I do love it.

I dreaded going into work the next day, though. I knew people wouldn't know what to say. It was the same when my parents died. Reactions were divided into two camps. Some people ignored that anything had happened, while others wanted to know every last detail. I started to feel as if my loss was filling a hunger in them and that they would eat me up if they could. As if all these bad things happening to me spared them.

I could see that my haircut worried everyone. Even as they were telling me how nice I looked, most were putting their hands up to their necks, checking that their hair was still there, that they were all right, that my misery hadn't leaped over to them. Like fleas.

❤ *See also Codes; Hair; Objects; Weight*

voices

Now that mine and John's telephone box has finally been pulled down, I am on a mission to keep others going for lovers everywhere. Every time I see one, I go in and ring someone up, although it can sometimes surprise them.

Recently, I've been ringing the number of my mother and father's house. It's been disconnected, and of course I know she won't, but I can't get rid of this hope that my mother will answer. I'm scared I'll forget what her voice sounded like. If I shut my eyes, I hear it very loud and screechy, saying things like, *No one's impressed by your misery, you know.* But then I try to listen with Sally's ears and it's different. It's not my father talking anymore, interpreting my mother for me.

I know there's a saying that you turn into your mother as you get older. Maybe everyone's the same. We're all trying to listen harder and harder to not just the words, but what our mothers were really saying to us all those years ago.

♥ *See also Codes; Daisies; Doors; Elephant's Egg; Telephone Boxes; Underwear; Vendetta; Washing Powder*

voyeur

Sally and I spent last Saturday shopping, for old times' sake. However, she didn't have any money and I could think of nothing I wanted to buy, so we just walked round in silence. Eventually, she had the idea that we should each buy the other a tattoo.

"What would you have?" I asked, and she said that she would have SALLY tattooed on her arm in beautiful rainbow colors, in case she forgot who she was.

"And me?" I asked.

"You'd have SALLY too, of course," she said. But then, because I looked so worried, she bought me a pair of novelty rainbow earrings made out of telephone wire instead.

I went to the loo to try them on when we went for coffee. I was in such a rush that I must have forgotten to shut the door, and just as I was putting the second one in, I looked up and saw a man standing in the doorway watching me through the mirror. He wasn't attractive—just an ordinary, middle-aged, tired-looking businessman—but he was watching me with such intensity that I felt we'd both been caught doing something far too intimate. He was just staring at me, running his fingers round his shirt collar, when our eyes locked, and my whole body turned to liquid. I don't know how long we stood there; we couldn't seem to look away. But suddenly, I froze, shut my eyes, and when I looked up, he'd gone. He'd even shut the door.

By the time I rejoined Sally, I was ready to shop. Only buying enough solid things would fill the gap that man had left in me. I didn't tell Sally. She thought I was relaxing at last and took advantage by picking out clothes that she knew I would never normally wear but that went with my new hairstyle. A fresh start, she kept saying. I even dragged her into the changing rooms with me. It wasn't just because we were having so much fun. I didn't want to be left alone with the mirror again.

❤ *See also Breasts; Indecent Exposure; Railway Stations; Wrists*

$\mathcal{W}$

washing powder

John hasn't been free to see me on the weekends for a long time now. There are times when I don't speak to anyone from the time I leave work on Friday to when I get back to the office on Monday morning. I have got so lonely, I have been known to ring the speaking clock just to hear the sound of someone else's voice.

But last week I had a bit too much to drink. On an impulse, I phoned the help line advertised on the side of the washing-powder box. The lady who answered was really friendly. And Scottish. I told her how I'd read somewhere that her company employed Scottish people because they sounded more like human beings, but she said it was because they were cheaper, and we laughed. We really did laugh together. Like friends do.

She asked me what machine I was using, and I said it was me that needed help. I told her how what I wanted most in the world was to be held. No one had held me for such a long time. I wanted to be hugged and washed and cleansed until I was white all over. That's when she told me I should call the Samaritans. I laughed and said they were just for unhappy people. Didn't she realize she was talking to someone who was so evolved, she'd once spent a week writing her obituary in order to guarantee happiness?

It was then that she said she was going to have to call her supervisor. There was no need for her to do that.

💜 *See also Friends; Happiness; Phantom E-mails; Wobbling; Yard*

weight

Sometimes I don't think my body can bear the weight of the pain that is being inflicted on it.

I've started to go to the gym just to build myself up. I want to be strong so that no one can push me around ever again. I want to weigh myself down so my feet stay on the ground. I want to become such a presence that everyone can see me. I don't ever want to become invisible.

Most of all, I want to matter.

💜 *See also Boxing; Codes; Gwyneth Paltrow; Kindness; Stepmothers; Youth*

what if . . .

- You could win a competition to be Queen for a year?
- It was a crime to have money?
- You woke up one morning and everyone was speaking a different language?
- There really were tiny little people living and working inside those machines, printing your passport photo, counting out your cash, and making your coffee?

- Children never grew up?
- You lived your life backward?
- You could make time stand still?
- Rich women went on a shopping strike?
- People stopped dying?
- John really had left Kate and married me?

❥ *See also Endings; Friends; True Romance; Utopia; Zest*

why?

S ally has agreed to listen to me talk about John on Friday evenings and Sunday lunchtimes, but only if I will cook for her. She says it's too much to cope with on an empty stomach.

I stand at the stove, stirring, while the tears run down my cheeks, and I press the bruise again and again. I go over every detail of our relationship—how we met, how John looked when he first kissed me, how I knew we were meant for each other, the connection we felt between us, and how I can't bear for it to be broken. Sometimes Sally will lean across and taste what I'm cooking, but mostly she'll just nod along. The funny thing is that she really does listen.

The other day I turned to her, and I could think of only one word to say. "Why?" I shouted it out.

She looked a bit frightened, which, despite my pain, made me want to laugh. "Why what?" she asked.

"Why wasn't I good enough for him?" I said. "Why didn't he want me?"

She shook her head. "You gave him up, Verity," she said. "It was you who finished it."

I sat down. I couldn't finish cooking the meal. I know I told John to go, but I didn't mean it. Surely Sally of all people could understand that. I suddenly saw that what had happened to me was exactly the same as with Colin and her. And all I'd wanted to do was to prove how different we were.

It was then that I decided to stop talking about John. He is now a closed book.

💜 *See also Endings; The Queen II; Sex; Ultimatum; Zeitgeist*

withdrawal

I read somewhere that in some parts of Japan, mothers breast-feed their babies for longer than we do in this country because they want to give their children the best possible start.

But when they decide enough is enough, they don't wean them off gently. One morning they paint their breasts with terrifying and horrific pictures and then wake the children up softly to take the breast just as before. The children are so filled with fright, they never want to feed from their mothers again.

This way, it is the child who has given up the breast and honor is satisfied on both sides.

💜 *See also Horror Movies; Ultimatum; Voices*

wobbling

The chairman has been on lots of courses aimed at positivity. If you ask him how he is these days, he no longer tells you he is surviving and starts patting his dog. Instead, he looks you in the eye and says he's fan-tas-tic or that everything is simply wonderful.

He has even taken to putting little quotes up in the reception area to buoy us up each day. Most people scoff at these, but Brian and I have become secretly addicted. We have taken to getting to work earlier and earlier just to see what today's quote will be. I think we're both looking for a message that will give us the clues we need to join the rest of the human race. We want to be winners too.

The other day I came in to find Brian had taped something to my computer. *Even if you are falling flat on your face, you are still moving forward,* I read.

Brian has been surprisingly kind to me. It is funny how it takes something dreadful happening to you to find out who your real friends are.

❤ *See also Codes; Dogs; God; Positive Thinking; Voices; Weight*

women's laughter

The only time I ever saw my father get angry with my mother was when she was helpless with laughter on the telephone once. He practically ran across the room, pulled the receiver from her hand, and slammed it down.

She just looked at him and laughed even louder, until he slapped her. He told me afterward that he didn't do it to hurt Mummy, but to stop her from getting hysterical.

I understood what he was saying at the time but probably even better now. Women's laughter is different from any other kind of laughter. It is louder, more generous, more absorbing and all-encompassing. It is as if they have forgotten other people exist. While women are laughing, they don't care about anybody else but one another. If some man tries to join in, the laughter dries up immediately, and the women bustle round getting busy with one of the hundreds of jobs they always seem to have to do.

I have a sneaking suspicion that if women laughed less, men might be happier.

♥ *See also Danger; Friends; Happiness; Imposter Syndrome; Lesbians; Victim*

woolworths

*A*fter the success of our last shopping expedition, Sally and I decided to spend Saturdays shopping in town. Last weekend she said she wanted to take me out for a special treat, and then she took me to Woolworths. I was surprised. When we were kids, during the summer holidays, we would tell our mothers that we were just going to the park near our estate, but then we'd jump on a bus and have baked beans on toast at the Woolworths in the center of town.

For dessert, we'd steal sweets from the "Pick 'n' Mix"

counter. We weren't the only ones. Even nowadays, you get adults looking at the sweets in Woolworths with a nostalgic look on their faces. They buy selections for their own children, but you can tell they think there's something unenterprising about this, something unnatural about just handing over the money. But then, children these days expect everything to fall on their plates without doing any of the work, don't they?

I was about to point this out to Sally when I saw the expression on her face. "I want you to get me a candy shrimp, a fruit chew, two pear drops, and a coconut mushroom," Sally said. For a few seconds, I thought about refusing, but there would be no point. I know Sally too well.

We ran down the street afterward, whooping and shrieking with joy. My hands were sweating so much that most of the sweets had disintegrated in them, but I didn't care. I kept looking into the faces of everyone passing me by, and just at that moment, it was as if Sally and I were the only ones who were truly alive.

♥ *See also Codes; Danger; Kindness; Women's Laughter; Zzzz*

words

Sometimes when I have a lot of work to type, I get confused over words. They start to look odd. I told Brian about this, and he agreed. We made a list of silly words together. *Eighth,* for instance, is completely ridiculous once you analyze it. So is *put.* Almost an insult.

We tried to write a letter together using every word on our list, but we had to give it up, we were laughing so much.

"You're all right sometimes, Ver," he said, which surprised me because he didn't then go on to make a joke about it. He's changed a lot since his warning. These days he's more like an unbounced Tigger. More manageable. He says the same about me.

What I didn't say to Brian—because he'd only get the wrong idea—is that one of the strangest words is *husband*. You can't help but break it into two syllables in your mouth. *Hus* is like a snake caught between your tongue and the top edge of your teeth. It makes your lips sneer to say it. And then *band* is almost dismissive. Draws your mouth back and lets any passion out without there being anything you can do about it. Say it carefully enough, and your lips are in exactly the right position to have a gag tied around so you can't utter another word.

This is something I wish I'd never discovered, because now I can't stop thinking about it.

♥ *See also other silly words in this lexicon: Ants; Ears; Gwyneth Paltrow; Lesbians; Noddy; Rude; Thrush; Ultimatum; Vendetta; Zen*

worst-case scenario

*B*rian says it's one step forward, two steps back. As soon as he got his work situation sorted out, his home life went to pot. It turns out his wife has been putting up with him only because she thought he'd collapse without her, but now she says he doesn't need her anymore. He said the funny thing is that he's been fearing this moment for such a long time, his first feeling was one of complete relief. It's as if he can start again.

I think of Sally. She says she will never trust another man again. She says that she doesn't need a man anymore. She says she is perfectly happy just being on her own. She says that she has saved up enough money from the time she was living off Colin so that she will never have to be dependent on anyone else ever again. She even says Colin has done her a favor.

It's humbling to think that the worst thing anyone can imagine is probably happening to someone, to some family, somewhere in the world right now. You can never be complacent. You can never just let things go on day after day without taking action, like Brian says he did.

♥ *See also Illness; Old; Utopia; Withdrawal*

wrists

The other day on the tube, there was a man standing up in front of me. He was holding on to that strap and reading his newspaper. I was just looking at the headlines, but then his wrist caught my attention.

I couldn't stop staring.

His wrist was beautiful. There is something about certain men's wrists just poking out of a jacket sleeve that gets me every time. That little nubble on the edge of the bone and the hollow in the middle of the flat bit that joins hand and arm. It's impossible to see a man with a wrist like that and not think of what he could do to you with his fingers.

I kept thinking what bit of my body had the same effect on John. It sounds strange, but I liked the backs of his knees best. It was as if no one else had ever touched them but me.

Sally has beautiful ears. When she's busy talking sometimes, she twists her hair behind her ears, and she looks like a little puppy dog. Her face is so sweet and vulnerable, I want to crush her to me. It's hard to explain, that mixture of wanting to hurt and wanting to care for someone all at the same time.

I was pleased when my station came and I could get off. Sometimes it's hard to realize how near to the edge you are standing.

♥ *See also Danger; Elephant's Egg; Nostrils; Railway Stations; Velvet*

xenophobia

My father hated going abroad. When my mother did manage to persuade him to go on a foreign holiday, he'd never be happier than when he found a view or a street that reminded him of the Home Counties.

"You could almost be in England," he'd say in admiration, and he would look around as if he'd found something remarkable. It used to drive my mother mad—the fact that he really did think that it was this that made going abroad worthwhile.

Sally and I have been planning lots of foreign holidays together. I phoned my solicitor to see how much money I had.

"Verity, your investments are so sound, you could practically buy the airline," he said, and when I started to say that I didn't really think I wanted to go that far, he interrupted to say he'd been joking.

"You really must take an interest," he said. "This is your future security we're talking about."

I pretended he was right, because I knew he'd only give me a lecture otherwise. I said that I'd start to read the business pages and get actively involved.

I even asked whether he'd help me understand it all a little better. He went all huffy and puffy and said he'd be delighted. He said that, even if he must say so himself, he'd been doing something rather clever and exciting with my capital investments that he thought I'd find rather amusing.

I told him I couldn't wait.

♥ *See also Ambition; Codes; Houses; Illness; Promotion; Voices; Yields*

x-rated

Colin rang me up at work. I was surprised but thought he'd called about Sally. I was all set to be a good best friend and put him straight about a thing or two, when he suddenly asked me if I wanted to have an affair with him.

I couldn't think of anything to say. Eventually, I said I was sorry.

"No harm in asking," he said and rang off.

I phoned Sally straightaway. I thought this was something she ought to know, and I'd rather she heard it from me than anyone else. I was surprised when she burst out laughing.

She said she'd been expecting something like this, just never thought it would happen so quickly. It was relief that made her laugh, she said. Relief that she didn't feel sadder about it. Sometimes you need to go as near to the edge as you can, for all the bad things you're imagining to pile up one on top of the other, so you can stop wondering about what might have happened. You know the worst.

"Typical Colin, though," she said then. "He's always had fantasies about the two of us, you and me."

When I put the phone down, I realized that Sally had painted a very different picture of what happened from what I think Colin was actually intending, but I suppose she's just trying to protect herself.

I had a long bath that night. Even if Sally was wrong, I wanted to wash off the feeling of being part of someone else's porn movie.

❤ *See also Colin; Lesbians; Phantom E-mails; Rude; Voyeur; Youth*

x-ray vision

S ally could be right about the fact that I have special powers. It's not something I like to talk about, but I am peculiarly sensitive to what people are really thinking. Gifts like this have to be used responsibly. Not everyone wants someone else looking inside their brain.

I have started to practice it with John. I sit cross-legged on the ground, hold a piece of his writing in be-tween my hands, and then I just concentrate.

I know when I connect with John because I feel this rush of energy surge through me and I get this picture in my mind like I'm this tiny little figure throwing herself on top of John and just clinging there. It does worry me that it always feels like this. As if I'm one of those monkey dolls hanging round a child's neck and not letting go.

I have to peel myself off before I can start to transmit thoughts to John. I tried it with Colin the other day. I thought of him replacing the receiver after I'd turned him down and saw how upset he was. The interesting thing was that Colin and I were walking hand in hand through a field of shining buttercups. I didn't do that clinging thing, and I was able to transmit to Colin easily. I felt he needed me, so I sent him healing thoughts.

Sometimes now when I use my powers, I'm not sure who is going to pop up—John or Colin. I don't do it so often anymore.

♥ *See also Omens; Sculpture; Teaching; Vendetta; Zest*

X

*T*here are things about Sally nowadays that keep reminding me of my mother. For instance, I had forgotten how strongly my mother believed in education. She was always attending classes at the local adult education center too. It was almost a religion with her. She'd search through the brochure every autumn, working out what to do. It was an interesting way to gain knowledge, because she became an expert on specialist subjects such as Stonehenge, garden history, and the Greek tragedies, but she was unable to add up a single row of figures. It was as if she were in training to become the perfect quiz-show contestant.

I found my grandparents' wedding certificate in my mother's drawer after she died. I was thinking about framing it when I noticed that my grandmother's father had signed with an X. I suddenly thought about my mother sitting at the kitchen table struggling over her books, and I felt so ashamed about how annoyed I was at the time because she was taking up so much space. I can't help wondering now what it must have been like in her house when she was growing up. Did they read books? How did she get to love reading so much? Is this why she was always buying books for me to read? I'd forgotten how many books she used to buy me, how we used to go to the library together every week.

If God had had a family, he'd have created a telephone number you could use for all those questions you

need to ask dead people once it's too late. A mobile with
wings.

♥ *See also Telephone Boxes; Voices*

Y

y a r d

The other night, I found myself walking down
Colin's road. This is not because he interests me. It
has become a habit from when he first took up with Sally.

I was surprised to see a milk bottle that had been
painted gold left out in the empty yard next door to
Colin's house. I couldn't imagine who had done such a
thing or why.

I often make observations like this. It's as if I am more
aware of what is going on around me than other people.
The other day, for instance, I saw a couple going round a
music shop filling up a basket each with CDs. Why was
that? Had they won the lottery? Or maybe they were both
starting music collections from scratch?

And then there was the old man on the train who was
composing a complicated musical score on the back of a
business letter. The businessman carrying a school satchel.
The middle-aged woman taking a rabbit for a walk in the
park with a collar and lead.

It's hard when the stories queue up like this and there's
no one to tell them to. I thought I might call Colin and tell
him about the milk bottle. It seems only polite since he

contacted me so recently and it was in his neighbor's yard.
I thought he might be interested.

❤ *See also Doors; Endings; Foreheads; Phantom E-mails;*
  Stalking; X-ray Vision

yellow

I have spent the weekend painting my hallway a cheerful yellow. It was exhausting, but I have rarely felt so
satisfied as when I finished. I kept going outside in the
street so I could open my front door and see how good it
looked.

I told Brian about it on Monday, and he said I'd created my own little sunlit island. I rushed home from work
just so I could see it again. I even left the door on the latch
so people walking past could glimpse in and feel jealous
of me and my home.

❤ *See also Doors; Property; Sculpture; Utopia; Washing Powder;*
  Wobbling

yields

S ally came round for supper to see my painting. I noticed that the conversation kept turning toward Colin
and that I blushed every time she mentioned his name, so
I tried to change the subject.

We started talking about Brian, and all our other
friends with disastrous love lives, but then we got back to
Colin again, so I asked Sally about her investments in-

stead. She has decided to keep her flat rented out and to buy another flat to live in. I was interested in this, because I'd been reading the papers like I promised the solicitor and there'd been several articles recently about the buy-to-let market in the suburbs. The solicitor keeps telling me that the yields we've been getting on my parents' house are disappointing, and although the tenants are safe, he wonders if I need to maximize my investments.

I thought about the last meeting I'd had with the solicitor, and I tried to practice some of the language I'd learned on Sally.

"It could be an idea," I told her, "to buy some property for short-term lets for all the people who have to move somewhere quickly when their relationships have broken down."

But then we couldn't stop talking. We planned out a hostel for the brokenhearted, with soundproof rooms so you could cry without anyone hearing you, enormous soft sofas to sink into, comfort food delivered to your door, country music piped into your bedroom, plastic bricks to throw at walls, and lots and lots of shoulders to lean on.

"Just like the song," she said. I could tell she thought it was just a bit of fun, but when she'd gone home, I started making notes. In the morning, I rang the solicitor and told him my mother's story about the architect and his lover. He said it sounded very interesting and made an appointment for me to come and see him to talk more about it.

♥ *See also Codes; Houses; Money; True Romance; Xenophobia; Youth*

you

I knew I shouldn't have done it. I knew it was a mistake even as I was dialing the number, but some time ago, I had written myself a note in my diary that today I could call John. Since then, I've been counting off the days. There were times when it was all that kept me going. However, even when I was waiting for him to answer, I was telling myself I'd never do it again. And then when he answered the phone and said, "Hello, you," I could tell he didn't know who it was for a second. He said he was pleased to hear from me and that he missed me, but I kept thinking about the way he'd said "Hello, you" and how different it was from every time he'd said it before.

When I put the phone down, I wrote another note in my diary for when I could call him again, but this is for a long time in the future. Anything could happen before then.

💜 *See also Grief; Mistaken Identity; Phone Calls; Why?*

youth

B rian read out a bit from the newspaper that said that men are genetically programmed to fall in love for a final but lasting time when they reach the age of fifty-one. What is interesting about this is that when John is fifty-one, I will be thirty-five and apparently, women of that age are often at their most fertile. This was the first thing I thought of, even though I haven't spoken to John for a

while. Still, it is nice to know we have ten more years before nature is ready for us if something should happen.

I eventually plucked up enough courage to call Colin.
He couldn't work out who I was at first, but then he suddenly burst out laughing.

"Verity," he said, as if I hadn't just been repeating my
name. "Sally's desperate friend."

I couldn't believe it. This is why I didn't stick up for
Sally when he told me that she had been too old for him.
That he was going out with an eighteen-year-old now. Evidently, they have a really strong connection, and she interests him in a way Sally never really could. "You know
what they say about younger chicks," he said with a
laugh, and then he asked me why I rang. I said I couldn't
remember.

Afterward, I told Brian what Colin had said. I thought
he might defend him, but he was disgusted.

"I guess that proves that some men are just genetically
programmed to be jerks," he said, and he put his arm
around me. He didn't even try to squeeze my waist like he
normally does.

Another interesting thing is that I remember Brian cel-
ebrating his fiftieth birthday last year.

❤ *See also Danger; Old; X-rated; Weight*

Z

zeitgeist

I'm finding it difficult to concentrate on reading anything substantial at the moment. All that happens is that I end up reading the same lines over and over again, watching the letters dance on the page rather than trying to take in the words.

To fill in the time, I've taken to doing the questionnaires in women's magazines. The strange thing is that they all seem to be about subjects I need the answers to. I have learned so much about myself as a result. I fill in those little boxes with as much concentration as my father used to tick off items on his list of things to do. My only worry is that I am slipping farther and farther down the age categories. I have noticed that in some magazines, there are no boxes to tick if you are over the age of thirty-four. Presumably by this stage, you will be too busy being successful to fill in questionnaires, but what happens if you don't manage that? How will you get to know things about yourself then?

❤ *See also Happiness; Illness; Imposter Syndrome; Routines; Teaching*

z e n

I can't remember how old I was when I realized that most things are better as memories than as the real thing.

It's the same with photographs. Everybody always smiles for the camera, so when you look back, it is difficult to imagine a more glorious time. This is why when people are looking through a pile of photographs and suddenly stop to look at one a bit harder, you know that it will be a picture of them. They are trying to remember what it felt like to be that happy and whether that moment was really more joyful than the unrecorded, soon-to-be-unremembered present moment.

♥ *See also Ants; Imposter Syndrome; Kindness; Mars Bars; Noddy; Velvet; Woolworths*

z e r o

I t's hard to pinpoint the exact time when work really did become something more than just a shield from the pain about John, but for the most part, it really is what I'm interested in nowadays.

There are even some days I can get through without crying.

I went to my first meeting as Brian's assistant the other day. The client said he was very impressed with our teamwork.

Brian took me out for a drink afterward and told me I was a natural. He then told me exactly how he was feeling and what he was going through. It took a long time, but it was just nice to be sitting in a pub with someone who wasn't looking over his shoulder the whole time or at his watch, wondering whether he had enough time to take you home. Or not.

"I needed a wake-up call," Brian said, "and speaking of which, what are you like in the morning?" As we left, Brian whispered: "We don't need to tell anyone at work about this, do we, Ver?" He kept calling me his little secret.

When Brian hugged me, it felt all wrong. I kept looking for spots to rest my head that just weren't there. His chin was bristly against my cheek, and I nearly passed out from how homesick I felt for John.

Brian's right about something, though. Sometimes you just have to keep moving forward. I rang the solicitor again when I got home. He said I should feel happy to contact him, night or day.

♥ *See also Imposter Syndrome; Phantom E-mails; Teaching; Victim; Youth; Zen*

z e s t

James, the solicitor, and I are opening the first of our brokenhearted hostels in six months' time. It's in my parents' old house, which is why we're calling it Rose's House. I think my mother would have liked that. The first of a bouquet of flowers, we hope.

It's like my life has started all over again. James says that with his experience and gravitas combined with my youth and energy, we make a perfect partnership. He loves listening to my stories. We've got very close during the planning stages, although I've been careful not to let the relationship go beyond business at the moment.

"I've learned the hard way," I tell him, "not to take anything for granted."

We've agreed that all the money I've invested in our brokenhearted-home scheme should be transferred into his name so he can handle the finances, leaving me free to concentrate on the creative planning and ideas. He's finally agreed that it's much better for both of us to do what we're best at. Now he's got to know me better, he's more trusting in our relationship.

It was worth the effort. James makes me feel completely protected. It is so wonderful not to have to worry about anything at all. For the first time in my life, I'm pleased to be me.

♥ *See also Daisies; Doors; Houses; Money—Even More of It; New Men; True Romance; Yellow*

zoology

Q: Why did the first monkey fall out of the tree?
A: *Because it was dead.*

Q: Why did the second monkey fall out of the tree?
A: *Because it was holding the first monkey's hand.*

Q: Why did the third monkey fall out of the tree?
A: *Because it thought it was a game.*

🖤 *See also Captains; Danger; Influences; Ultimatum; Why?*

Z Z Z Z

I woke up in the night realizing that the poets I read when I was a teenager had got it wrong.

Love's not like a roller coaster because of the ups and downs. It is more because you queue up for hours to get on the ride, then you are strapped in, so you can't get out even when you're about a third of the way through and realize you've changed your mind. There's nothing you can do, you've just got to carry on until the end, and even then, you've got to wait until someone else releases you and says you can go.

And once you're safely back on solid ground, you're rushing off to join the next queue.

Luckily, I went back to sleep, and by the time the alarm went off, I'd come to my senses and forgotten all about this.

I remembered only when Sally told me that she feels now that living with Colin made her feel like she was strapped to a chair watching her life go by. I didn't tell her my theory. She'd have only related it to the solicitor or something silly like that.

Sally's going to be my date to the opening party for our hotel. She laughed when I told her that I wanted one room to be just like her parents' spare room, but after all, that was where I used to imagine myself when I was suffering the most after John. I haven't told Sally how I've kept that velvet scrap in my pocket the whole time. It's nearly worn out now.

Sally said she always wanted to live in my house. She said she used to secretly pretend my mother was hers.

It made me think. I want each room in my hotel to be decorated like a different dream of home. After all, home is like love. It's just a state of mind, a fantasy, that you can learn to live without if necessary.

I'm not going to invite anyone else to the party. Just Sally.

Money—Even More of It; Mystery
Tours; Nursing; Old; Phantom E-mails;
The Queen II; Utopia; Withdrawal

Entrepreneurs   Ambition; Best Friends; Firefighting;
Kisses; Money—Even More of It; Ob-
jects; Promotion; Ultimatum; Yields;
Zest

Fathers   Ambition; Ants; Houses; Illness; Lust;
Mistaken Identity; Orphans; Out-
cast; Poverty; Routines; Thomas the
Tank Engine; True Romance; Voices;
Women's Laughter; Xenophobia

Gastronomic   Baked Beans; Crème Caramel; Elephant's Egg; Ice Cream; Liqueur
Chocolates; Mars Bars; Oranges

Homes   Doors; Houses; Magazines; Noddy;
Objects; Property; True Romance;
Utopia; Velvet; Yellow

Image   Boxing; Breasts; Codes; Danger; Fashion; Glitter; Gwyneth Paltrow; Happiness; Indecent Exposure; Mirrors;
Mustache; New Men; Normals; Old;
Outcast; The Queen; Start-rite Sandals; Underwear; Visible; Voyeur;
Weight; Wrists

John	See every entry in the alphabet
Kate	*Kate; Lesbians; Letters; Old; Reasons . . . ; Stalking*
Lust	*Breasts; Fat Women; Ice Cream; Indecent Exposure; Jacuzzi; Kisses; Marathons; Objects; Phone Calls; Rude; Stationery; Thomas the Tank Engine; Toys; Vexed; Voyeur; Wrists*
Mothers	*Daisies; Elephant's Egg; Engagement Ring; Heroines; Houses; Illness; Influences; Mirrors; Mistaken Identity; Positive Thinking; Quick; Stepmothers; True Romance; Underwear; Velvet; Voices; Withdrawal; Women's Laughter; X; Zest*
Names	*Daisies; Glenda G-spot; Names; Normals; Surnames; Words; You*
Outsiders	*Ants; Captains; Daisies; Fat Women; Mistaken Identity; Money; Noddy; Outcast; The Queen; Revenge; Stalking; Unfit; Vendetta; Voyeurs; Washing Powder; Withdrawal; X*
Personal Development	*Ambition; Boxing; Dreams; Endings; God; Happiness; Heroines; Horror*

Movies; Imposter Syndrome; Kind-
ness; Omens; Pain Index; Positive
Thinking; Teaching; Weight; Wobbling;
X; Zeitgeist

Relations   Baked Beans; Blood; Daisies; Danger; Elephant's Egg; Illness; Mirrors;
Mistaken Identity; Only Children; Orphans; Relatives; Stepmothers; Underwear; Zzzz

School   Blackbirds, Robins, and Nightingales;
Blood; Captains; the Fens; Mars Bars;
Outcast; Telephone Boxes; Woolworths

Telephones   Marathons; Phone Calls; Surnames;
Telephone Boxes; Washing Pow-
der; Women's Laughter; X-rated;
Yard; Yields; Youth; Zero; Zest

Unfairness   Ants; Baked Beans; Blackbirds, Robins,
and Nightingales; Crème Caramel; Dan-
ger; Doors; God; Mystery Tours;
Noddy; Quick; Thrush; Ultimatum; Vendetta; Victim; Why?; Withdrawal; Youth; Zoology

Vengeance   Ants; Dogs; Engagement Ring; Letters;
Mistaken Identity; Nursing; Old; Revenge; Zest

Women   *Ambition; Boxing; Breasts; Fat Women; Glenda G-spot; Glitter; Gossip; Heroines; Lesbians; Mustache; Old; Sex; Stationery; Toys; Underwear; Voices; Weight; Withdrawal; Women's Laughter*

about the author

Sarah Salway lives in Kent with her husband and two children and is a prize-winning short-story writer and poet. *The ABCs of Love* is her first novel.